D1490611

# A Boring
# Wife
# Settles
# the Score

Marie-Renée Lavoie

Translated by Arielle Aaronson

ARACHNIDE

First published in French as *Diane demande un recomptage* in 2020 by Les Éditions XYZ
First published in English in Canada in 2021 and the USA in 2021
by House of Anansi Press Inc.
www.houseofanansi.com

House of Anansi Press is committed to protecting our natural environment. This book is made of material from well-managed FSC®-certified forests, recycled materials, and other controlled sources.

House of Anansi Press is a Global Certified Accessible™ (GCA by Benetech) publisher. The ebook version of this book meets stringent accessibility standards and is available to students and readers with print disabilities.

25 24 23 22 21    1 2 3 4 5

Library and Archives Canada Cataloguing in Publication

Title: A boring wife settles the score / Marie-Renée Lavoie ; translated by Arielle Aaronson.
Other titles: Diane demande un recomptage. English
Names: Lavoie, Marie-Renée, 1974– author. | Aaronson, Arielle, translator.
Description: Translation of: Diane demande un recomptage.
Identifiers: Canadiana (print) 20200371428 | Canadiana (ebook) 20200371495 | ISBN 9781487009373 (softcover) | ISBN 9781487009380 (EPUB) | ISBN 9781487009397 (Kindle)
Classification: LCC PS8623.A8518 D5313 2021 | DDC C843/.6—dc23

Text design: Sara Loos
Typesetting: Lucia Kim

*House of Anansi Press respectfully acknowledges that the land on which we operate is the Traditional Territory of many Nations, including the Anishinabeg, the Wendat, and the Haudenosaunee. It is also the Treaty Lands of the Mississaugas of the Credit.*

**Canada Council Conseil des Arts for the Arts du Canada**

ONTARIO ARTS COUNCIL
CONSEIL DES ARTS DE L'ONTARIO
an Ontario government agency
un organisme du gouvernement de l'Ontario

With the participation of the Government of Canada
Avec la participation du gouvernement du Canada | Canada

*We acknowledge the financial support of the Government of Canada through the National Translation Program for Book Publishing, an initiative of the Action Plan for Official Languages — 2018–2023: Investing in Our Future, for our translation activities.*

Printed and bound in Canada

# A Boring
# Wife
# Settles
# the Score

# 1

## In which I do a little math

Life is much too complex for a person's age to accurately reflect the number of years they've lived. Merely adding up the days seems to me outrageously simplistic. A ten-year-old stuck in a war-torn country is ancient. An old person who has spent a lifetime navelgazing is basically a teenager in a wrinkly body. For decades, plenty of adults have lingered over the saccharine joys of adolescence with nobody keeping an eye on the stopwatch. Humans evolve in dimensions that exist beyond the laws of time, math be damned. Poor Einstein.

I know a few people in their fifties (insert name here) who have yet to mature beyond age twenty or so. Occasionally, the people we think are flush with wisdom and therefore immune to the whims of youth take prodigious — and completely unexpected — leaps backward, landing on a snake and tumbling down the board. These regressions are as common as a cold, and though shrinks have formulated a great number of theories with complicated names to explain the phenomenon, I believe this theorizing attributes an overblown sense of importance to it. The regressions are nothing more than brain farts settling in toxic miasmas over everyone around.

Yet for these men and women, as for everyone else, time marches on, undistracted. Which makes sense: for society to run smoothly, people, like cars, can exist only as a function of their age. We need to be able to rank them, collect statistics, and set insurance premiums. But I've done the math and I've decided that the shadow cast by the big five-oh, hovering over me since my last birthday, is cruelly lacking in nuance.

# 2

## In which I treat my feet
## and eat cassoulet

My family doctor died. Doctors die like everyone else, the poorly shod shoemakers. You can't evade the Grim Reaper like the taxman, can't worm your way out of dying. Everyone has to pay their dues. Pity, though. He was a good soul and should have earned a deferral. I say that very selfishly.

While I waited to be assigned to someone new, I put my faith in the good graces of a walk-in clinic taking NFD ("no family doctor") patients of all stripes adding to the burden of a system already struggling with our extended lifespans. But I couldn't take it anymore. I had to do something about my desiccated feet, their heels cracked and bleeding. The ointments and creams I'd bought on everyone's recommendation hadn't done a thing. The dry patch dried some more and grew, threatening to spread to the rest of my body, already lying fallow since Jacques had left me.

As I sat in a waiting room full of people who seemed sicker than me, I started questioning the urgency of my visit. I remember feeling the same way any time one of the kids was hurt. Between arriving at the clinic in a panic — a worried mother making loud and forceful demands — convinced that my child required immediate care, and hearing our name called over the PA, my conviction would transform itself into the belief that I was unnecessarily bogging down the system and stealing an appointment from someone who was *truly* sick. Everyone knows kids always feel better once they're in the waiting room. On this day, when I realized that it would take several hours for A-74 to be called, I was initially furious — *half my taxes go to health care, for crying out loud!* — until I remembered, just before turning into a cranky old woman, that I hadn't paid taxes since being laid off a few months earlier. So I dutifully sat and waited. It's not like I had anywhere else to go.

The man sitting opposite me was sound asleep, arms crossed, lower lip hanging. It was only a matter of time before he started drooling. I've always been amazed by just how easily men sleep in public. They're able to doze off in a crowd, whether at a meeting, in the middle of a baptism or a play, or at a Senate assembly. At the last Chamber of Commerce gala I'd been to, one of the deputy ministers fell asleep onstage. But instead of being offended, people look at them tenderly ("Just let him be, the poor man's tired."). Women, however, rarely if ever sleep in public. They're too busy keeping up appearances, an obsession they've been saddled with since childhood and that compels them to poison themselves for the rest of their lives. We rush to wake women when they doze off inadvertently ("We can't let her look crazy!") and anticipate their excuses ("I was just resting my eyes."). It's always the same old story: women who drink, smoke, and snooze on the job are vulgar and weak, but men who indulge in the same things are *real* men. The day we truly address gender equality is the day we think it's cute when a woman nods off at a family party. My daughter, Charlotte, doesn't think we'll make any progress so long as women keep saying "*my* housework isn't done" instead of "*the* housework isn't done."

By the time my number was called, my phone had been dead for an hour and a half and I'd paged through all the tattered gossip magazines lying around. I hadn't learned anything of substance, other than that celebrities marry and unmarry more frequently than regular people do and that the Kardashians make a lot of babies—oh, and that Demi Moore has saggy knees. I bet her plastic surgeon has since resolved the aesthetic issue that threatened to label her a dog.

I was directed toward a small examination room, where a young nurse came to check my blood pressure, pulse, and weight.

"Is my weight really necessary?"

"Have you stepped on a scale recently?"

"Uh…no."

Obviously, like all women who wished they didn't give a damn, I knew how much I weighed to the ounce. I just didn't want to say it out loud, to hear it echo against the beige walls of the broom closet where—I probably should have said as much—I'd only come for a miracle foot cream. But I'm a good sport, so I stripped down and closed my eyes as I stepped onto the obnoxious scale. Denial is just another form of defense. I couldn't have been more than twenty-five pounds from happiness, so what point was there in ruining my day?

"Are you running a fever?"

"No."

"What are you here for?"

"My heels."

"Your heels?"

"Yes."

"What seems to be the problem?"

"They're so dry they've started to crack and bleed all over. They aren't too painful, but I look like a leper when

I go out like this. I've tried every cream imaginable."

She was taking notes with codes and abbreviations, as if the bloody heel branch of medicine had its own jargon. I should have told myself I was in good hands, but instead I just felt foolish. A tattoo of small interwoven flowers encircled her wrist and disappeared beneath the sleeve of her uniform. Maybe her back was covered with a tangle of indiscreet stems thrusting their flowers into her body's most intimate folds.

"Any other issues?"

"Oh, lots, but nothing medical."

She smiled politely, like when someone asks a waitress what she ate "to get so pretty." Funny, old woman, real funny.

The doctor entered a few minutes later looking altogether unimpressed, as if he was already aware I'd come in for something silly. He was greying around the temples, his eyes were marked by crow's feet, and he had the deep facial furrows of someone who could stand to gain a few pounds. He was easily pushing sixty. I imagined him slouched in a wing chair, its carved legs sitting on a bearskin rug, a glass of bourbon in one hand.

"Ms. . . . Delaunais?"

"That's right."

"So this is about your . . . heels?"

"Yes, the ones on my feet."

"Well, that's good, I don't know of any other kind."

"Hah."

"Have a seat, little lady."

"I'm sure it's no big deal, I just want a prescription-strength cream. My heels are so dry they keep cracking and bleeding all the time, and the over-the-counter stuff isn't working."

I climbed the stepstool and lowered my little-lady bum onto the white paper I hoped was clean. Just the thought of sitting on discharge left by other patients made my stomach turn. I was wearing the skinny jeans I'd bought with Charlotte the year before, which made it difficult to lift my leg and show him the back of my right foot, the worse of the two.

"Let's take a look."

"Of course it's not bleeding now, I haven't done much today..."

"That's enough, you can put your shoes back on."

"Oh! Already? You had enough time to—"

"Uh-huh."

He was already writing something in my file. Some gibberish in an illegible cursive. If I'd known it would be this easy, I would have simply sent a photo.

"It seems like you're familiar with this... Does it have a name?"

"Housewife syndrome."

He said it like you'd spit out a hair stuck to your

tongue, shrugging his shoulders ever so slightly as if to say, *Let's call a spade a spade.*

"Women who don't work never wear socks. They walk around all day in slippers or sandals. Their skin doesn't have a chance to rehydrate, so it dries out and cracks over time."

His words, buoyed by an undercurrent of scorn, conjured up a list of offensive "synonyms" for the gender term in question — small fry, unpaid nanny, second-class citizen, woman who looks like something the cat dragged in — that fortunately drowned out the life-saving image of the sledgehammer I kept in the front hall closet for emergencies such as this. Knowing it was in close reach had a calming, reassuring, Gandhifying effect.

"Here's a prescription for a cream. Apply it morning and evening, and wear socks two or three days a week. It won't take long for you to see results."

I allowed myself one tiny act of vengeance, a childish one that did me a world of good. He needed an Ethics 101 class to understand that it took a shamefully narrow mind to equate "housewife" with "woman who doesn't work," but nevertheless I settled for a compliment as I was leaving.

"It's very noble of you to continue practising medicine, even past retirement age. We're in such need of frontline doctors."

The smile he offered in response was strangely similar to the kind my friend Claudine reserves for her daughter Adèle at her most infuriating. In teen-speak, rife with scatological references some kids never grow out of, it's called a "need-to-shit smile." I said goodbye, waving the white flag with my prescription. Whatever you do, seek peace. That's what I taught the kids.

Out in the waiting room, the man was still sleeping, his D-49 ticket clasped between his thumb and index finger. D-53 was blinking on the screen. A sleeping man is so adorable.

I met Claudine at La Casserole, a cute little French bistro a stone's throw away from the duplex we'd bought together a few months after my separation. She lived on the ground floor with her daughter Adèle — Laurie, her older daughter, had since moved in with her boyfriend. I was on the second floor with Cat-in-the-box, a.k.a. Steve, my three-legged pet, who was unafraid of the stairs. The bistro's cassoulet had healing properties that could mend most of life's misfortunes, and in just a few months we'd used it to repair our broken hearts and souls so often that our waistlines had expanded — we'd burn the weight off in spin class or boot camp at some point or another.

"There must be an actual name for it! You should have sent him packing."

"I did one better..."

"Hey! Before I forget—happy-hour Thursday night at Igloo."

"Eh..."

"Oh come on, J.P. will be there."

"So what? He's married!"

"He's still fun to look at."

"That just annoys me more than anything."

"Oh come! The new guy should be there, too."

"Fabio?"

Claudine couldn't imagine making out with a Fabien, so we'd changed his name slightly to give it a sexier feel. The server arrived carrying our steaming stoneware bowls on a thick wooden board.

"Watch out, ladies!"

The exposed parts of the ham shoulder, salt pork, sausages, and duck confit had gently browned to perfection inside the wood-fired oven. A thin, greasy film covered the bean stew, and I was ready to plunge my fork between the pieces of carrot and utterly sacrilegious leeks—I once saw a French tourist crossing himself at the sight—the better to savour the aroma's meaty swirls through my nose. Claudine's daughters, unwaveringly vegetarian, refused to set foot in the place as the smells alone would lead them to betray their convictions. My salivary glands were working in overdrive, helping to break down the molecules of such an unholy (but Lord, how exquisite!) quantity of calories. The downside: I'd never make it to the Paris-Brest dessert.

"Should I bring you another glass of Cahors?"

"No choice, I'm afraid."

Paradoxically, with a glass of "fat-cutter" (as our host liked to call it) to highlight the wine's utility, the meal seemed less decadent — reasonable, almost; the liquor was more than an accompaniment to the dish, it also served as a remedy. And we were good patients.

"So, how about you?"

"Shitty day."

"Oh."

"I just got back from Adèle's school."

"Oh boy . . ."

"The fruit of my womb is suspended for three days."

"ALREADY? The school year just started!"

"She wears frayed jeans that aren't permitted, crop tops that aren't permitted, shoes with wheels that aren't permitted, and she talks to her teachers just like she talks to me. To give you some idea . . ."

"Shoes with wheels?"

"Her dad brought them back from the States. Perfect if you feel like falling on your ass or splitting your head open. So after nine warnings, two detentions, and a few poorly-chosen-but-heartfelt *fuck offs*, they decided to suspend her."

"They're patient."

"Very."

"What're you going to do?"

"Not sure yet."

"Take her phone away?"

"Her father confiscated it Saturday."

"What for?"

"Her bad attitude, is what he told me."

"Man, what's going on with her?"

"I thought about the wheel of torture, but I don't have a wheel big enough. Being drawn and quartered is apparently pretty excruciating, but I'd need horses and I don't feel like moving to the countryside just for that."

"What about burning her at the stake?"

"Where'd we do it?"

"Out in the alley."

"The fire station is down the street. The guys will come running even before I get the flames going. They're obsessed with their response times, the bunch of maniacs."

"Chinese water torture?"

"Don't know how."

"Me neither."

"I thought about ice baths, like they used to have at the insane asylums—"

"That sounds horrible."

"—but she's too heavy, I'd never get her in. She'd put up a fight, land a few kicks. It wouldn't end well."

"Time to call in the artillery."

"What were you thinking?"

"When was the last time your mother saw her darling grandbabies?"

"Oh my God…"

## 3

### In which I struggle to jump back
### into the food chain

"They'll probably ask you to do some role-playing, so let's practise."

"I doubt that's necessary. I have plenty of experience with kids and almost graduated from college..."

Once again, I had to dive into the chaos surrounding me. I needed to get a job—the doctor's petty jibe had gotten to me—but there was no way I was working a nine-to-five gig in an air-conditioned cubicle with a Josy-Josée (the generic term for a gossipy office snoop who stirs up trouble, the kind of assistant you want to throw your coffee at), or busting my ass selling anything to anyone. I didn't want to be chained to a computer, or have my time and energy exploited for the financial edi-fication of a handful of shareholders already glutted like overfed geese. I wanted to make a valuable contribution, to devote body and soul to a worthy cause, to help those in need and—pardon the cliché—make a difference. To my daughter, Charlotte, who'd listened to my new existential musings and knew my pathetic resumé by heart, one word towered above the rest, lofty as a cathedral: *school*. The word alone is synonymous with multifaceted dedication, the ultimate self-sacrifice (from which the state benefits substantially), and personal satisfaction (a positive sentiment that ennobles the state's savings).

School is a bottomless pit of needs to be filled, of wounds of all sizes to nurse, desires to supervise, wonders to spark. The investment is direct, human, and uncompromising. Working in a school inspires admiration, and who minces their words, stitched together in appreciation (and with unmistakable pity), when faced with people taking on such a profession?

"Mom, you can't treat the kids at school like your own children, this isn't the 1900s. There are lots of things you're not allowed to do anymore."

"Like what?"

"Slap them on the wrist."

"Sometimes you don't have a choice."

"But you can't, that's what I'm telling you! You'll get in trouble! You'll have the administration, parents, and social media all over you if you do."

"Okay, then. Shoot."

"Mrs. Delaunais…"

"That would be me."

"Don't overdo it, just nod a little and say *uh-huh*."

"Why?"

"Because otherwise you sound old-fashioned, out of touch. And besides, that's not how you talk in real life. Just act natural, okay? So. Why do you want to work in our Before and After School program?"

"Because if I stay home all day, I'll dry up like an old middle-class divorcée…"

"Mom…"

"Because I live down the street."

"…"

"Because I love children and I want to give back to the community. And because I live down the street, it's convenient."

"Let's do a little role-playing, Mrs. Delaunais."

"Uh-huh."

"Two children start squabbling during recess and the fight turns physical. How do you handle the situation?"

"Is one of them bleeding?"

"It doesn't matter."

"It does in hockey — four minutes and not two if you are."

"*Mom…*"

"I'm kidding, sweetheart."

"Very funny."

"I separate them and tell them to have a think."

"About what?"

"Whatever they want, as long as they pretend to be sorry afterwards."

"Mom!"

"What do you want them to think about? They're pissed off at each other! Apologizing in front of everyone is only for show. Kids don't think about their behaviour, all they think about is getting even. Every parent knows that."

"But you can't *say* that!"

"You told me to be myself."

"Oh, forget it. Here's another one: Mrs. Delaunais, what do you do if a child wets his pants?"

"I pretend not to notice."

"He comes over to you crying."

"I send him to the locker room to shower and change his clothes."

"We don't have showers, this is an elementary school."

"Then I clean him up with brown paper towels as best as I can and have him put on clean clothes."

"What if the child doesn't have any?"

"Then we'll go through the lost and found."

"Too easy. But good point."

"But he'll smell like pee, so the other kids will pick on him. It'll end in a squabble, so we're back to the first situation with the same solution: the kid full of pee in one corner, the mean kids in the other, both pretending to have a think."

"Mom…"

"That's how most fights usually start, believe me. I've seen enough of them."

"A little girl comes to school half dressed in the dead of winter?"

"We go back to the lost and found, then call her parents and yell at them."

"A student shows up without a lunch?"

"I find the little brat who drew blood earlier, then take his lunch and give it to the hungry student."

"…"

"Just kidding. Everyone donates a little of their own lunch. Then we call the parents and yell at them."

"You find out that one of your students is being bullied by a bunch of mean kids."

"I find out who the ringleader is and take him out."

"…"

"We call the victim's parents and suggest they hire hit men to quietly eliminate the ringleader, ideally not on school property."

I may be boring (as harsh as they'd been at the beginning of our separation, my ex-husband Jacques's words now amuse me), but sometimes I do think I'm very funny.

"Well, I can't listen to your little comedy routine all day, I have other things to do."

"OKAY OKAY! I'll be serious: we notify everyone—the other aides, the teachers, parents, administration, psychologists—and we form an intervention team to meet with the bullies and the victim, either together or separately, to try to break the pattern of unhealthy behaviour. We set strict conditions for the bullies that could lead to their suspension or even expulsion. We lead activities to raise awareness with the other students, we destigmatize, we talk, we do educational workshops, projects, 3-D mobiles, hire celebrities to come talk to the kids…"

"Whoa! You're on a roll, don't stop now."

"And if a little girl is crying because she misses her mom and feels all alone, I wrap her in a hug and do my best to comfort her by whispering lots of reassuring things."

My Charlotte tilted her lovely head twenty degrees north-northwest, and I knew that if it were up to her I'd have the job, bad jokes and all. Tucked away in the golden section of her memory was an image of gentle Clarisse, who had kindly offered up her arms and her pillowy breasts during those first days of kindergarten until the separation eased. I had neither her generous shape nor her patience, but I did have a knack for making children love me. Worst-case scenario, there'd be a secret stash of candy waiting.

• • •

The school secretary didn't say a word. Instead, she held up a sheet of paper with "BREAK" written across it in large letters.

"Oh! No problem, I'll sit down and wait. I'm here to apply for the After School position."

"I'm sorry," the woman said. "I don't have a choice. Otherwise it never stops—the parents, the phone calls, the deliveries, the kids who've hurt themselves, kindergarteners who aren't potty trained—whatever, it just doesn't stop. Classrooms are full, the school's overflowing, and right now the principal is teaching because we're down a teacher. The substitute left yesterday in tears—second one since the school year started—and the janitor had to finish out the day."

I glanced at the calendar by the door: September 17.

"Sometimes the cleaning can wait. At least, it does at my house, and I bet it's the same in lots of other homes. Not everyone can afford a cleaning lady. I mean, I probably could, it just depends on your priorities. Me, I like clothes—I'd rather buy clothes and clean up after myself. And besides, the toilet really should be scrubbed every few days, but who's gonna get a cleaning lady to come that often? So the cleaning can wait, that's what I think. A dirty house never killed anyone, did it? We've

all been there and we're not any worse off if the janitor watches over a class once in a while, just to help
out. The cleaning can wait, that's what I say, same as
everywhere."

I was impressed; despite her chattiness, she still managed to finish a thought. Under the harsh neon lights,
the bubble-gum-pink highlights some hairdresser had
thought would be a good idea to sprinkle over her head
swept the air like a feather duster, though they could
have been — well, no, after I had a better look, almost
certainly were — the result of a home dye-job. I couldn't
pin down her age, likely somewhere between thirty-five
and fifty-five. She talked like a busybody and sounded
like a grandmother in the body of a potato slowly going
to seed, and now that she was done vigorously stirring her yogurt with a clear plastic spoon ("pre-stirred,"
it stated right on the label), she started to talk again,
churning the words out in milky consonants.

"I never get to drink my coffee while it's hot. Never
never never never. From the second I walk in the door,
that's it, *finito*, not a minute to myself until I leave for
the day. Not even to pee! Yesterday I had a teacher follow me into the bathroom to say she was bringing me
a kid who was feeling sick. We had to talk over the stall
door to figure out what to do with him, just to give you
an idea. I didn't even have my pants pulled up before
the kid puked outside my office. Good thing the janitor

wasn't in a class at the time, some messes can't wait..."

A student walked in holding both hands to his forehead, moaning like he was dying. The secretary rolled her eyes so far back they ricocheted off the ceiling before landing on the poor kid, who'd instinctively turned toward me. The "housewife" vibe, no doubt.

"*My head hurts...*"

"The secretary's taking a little break, it won't be long. Why don't you let me look at it in the meantime? Oh dear, that's some bump! What happened?"

"I bent over and so did Cedric."

"You both bent over at the same time?"

"I dropped my spinner."

"Your what?"

"My spinner!"

"I bet he just wanted to help."

"No, he wanted to steal it!"

"Now then, you shouldn't accuse someone like that."

"He's always stealing my stuff!"

"Okay, okay. Let's go put some cold water on that boo-boo. You can show me where the bathrooms are."

"But I lost my spinner!"

"What do you even do with a spinner?"

"You spin it."

"Where's your spinner now?"

"Miss Valérie took it."

"And Cedric wasn't hurt?"

"No. His head is hard."

The secretary hadn't moved a muscle. Her entire being had retreated into the glowing rectangle of her phone, forgetting the cup of coffee cooling at her side.

"Do you mind if I take him to the bathroom?"

"What class are you in, kiddo?"

"Miss Valérie's."

"What's your name?"

"Luis Sanchez."

"Ah, I should have known, with a tan like that! Lucky kid. Go ahead while I finish my break."

Kidnapping a child is easier than you think.


The school was under construction. Some of the walls had been gutted, others hid their bare bones behind plastic sheets. Piles of building materials spilled into the hallways. In such a narrow space, a horde of panicked children running from a fire would have been trampled in a heartbeat. My maternal instincts bristled slightly.

"You can't come in. This is the boys' bathroom."

"Moms are allowed."

"You're a mom?"

"Yes, I have three children. One girl and two boys."

"What are their names?"

"Charlotte, Antoine, and Alexandre."

"What class are they in?"

"They're all grown up now, they have jobs. Well, Charlotte's still in school, but...it's complicated."

"Are you a grandma?"

"Uh...not yet. Let's take some of the brown paper towel, here...and some cold water...just a sec...hey, this one isn't working...this one isn't either..."

A section of human wall had just appeared in the door frame, helmeted and weighed down with a huge leather belt brimming with tools of all kinds. A section of wall with dimples drilled into its cheeks, no beard, and no visible tattoos. An old-timer whose weathered face appeared to have gained a few years on his body.

"Water's off, sorry about that. There's a cooler at the end of the hall if you need a drink."

"Oh!"

"We're turning it back on in five."

"It's for the little guy's head, he had a bit of an accident."

"Oh, boy! Nasty bump you got there."

"I banged heads with Cedric."

"Better put ice on that."

"I doubt I'll find any here."

"I'll give you one of my ice packs. Are you his teacher?"

"No, no...I...work" (in my head I was using the future tense) "for the Before and After program. My name's Diane."

"Jim."

We followed Jim over to a big red Coleman cooler that looked as if it had been used as a sawbench. Inside was enough food for an army: yogurt, carrot sticks, a couple of kilos of trail mix, some sandwiches, a few clementines, a bag of cheese curds, and more. It reminded me of when Antoine was a teenager and I had to make him two lunches because he couldn't help eating the first one during morning recess.

"Diane?"

Behind me, another man's voice—and the feeling that I'd heard it before. It took me a few seconds to place him because his hair was shorter and a long-sleeved shirt hid his tattoos.

"Guy?"

"Hey, hey! You're a teacher now?"

"No! No, no..."

"Then what are you doing here?"

"I could ask you the same thing! I thought you only did residential..."

"One of my friends recruited me. It's a change from the whiny clients and the while-you're-at-its. You still in the same place?"

With his gigantic hands, Jim was showing the boy how to press the ice against his head.

"No, I sold. I bought a duplex three blocks from here with a friend. Actually, you know her. Remember the one who broke her arm? You brought us to the hospital last year..."

"Oh yes, *Flashdance!*"

Recalling the scene and our boozy old-lady faces, I wasn't convinced it was a good thing he had remembered so quickly. Fortunately, the boy had brought his ice pack over and was hanging on to my leg, giving me a little credibility and painting me in what I hoped was a more attractive light.

"Did you say thank you to Jim, Luis?"

"I think so."

"We'll put the ice pack in your cooler when we're done, Jim."

"Great!"

"Well, I gotta go up, we're turning the water back on. I'll see you again, we're here until the holidays, at least." Guy put his hand on my shoulder before he walked away, smiling. "Glad to see you're doing well."

The stairwell had swallowed him up by the time I managed to squeak out a "Me, too." A gentle warmth radiated from the brief imprint left by his fingers. It had been a while since I'd been touched.

Seconds later, the bell for recess rang, unleashing a tsunami of children eager to cut loose in the single corner of the schoolyard unaffected by the construction. The clamour of small voices was drowned out by shouts of "In line!"; "No running on the stairs!"; and

"Quietly!" Were it not for the promise of seeing Guy again, I might have run away myself.

Gripping the handset of one of the last corded phones in history, the secretary wagged a stern index finger, instructing a student to wait until she was finished. A woman in a pantsuit burst into the office at the same time, visibly out of breath.

"Ah! You're the substitute!"

"Uh, no ... I'm here for—"

She pivoted to the secretary, giving off a faint whiff of sweat.

"Lucie! Is the substitute coming?"

The secretary shook her head no.

"Arrrgh!"

Luis had gone back to class in the hopes of getting his spinner back—that, or exacting revenge on the kid who had made him lose it. It was clear how things would end. The lump on his forehead looked like a third arm was trying to poke its way through. I fiddled with the lukewarm ice pack to occupy my hands. Pantsuit turned to me.

"'Scuse me, ma'am, but we're up to our eyeballs right now."

"I can tell, no problem."

"Are you a mom?"

"No. Yes, but I'm here about the Before and After School program."

"You'll need to see Andrée about that. End of the hall-way on the left. Are you sure you're not a substitute?"

"What kind of credentials do you need to be a sub-stitute?"

"For this class, a tenth-dan black belt would do."

She winked at me before running off. The secretary finally turned to the little boy who was waiting his turn to speak.

"Okay, what is it you want, honey?"

"Uh... I forget."

"I see you have a note with you, it must be for me."

"Oh yeah!"

My interview with Andrée didn't last long. Judging by her vigorous nodding, my answers seemed satis-factory. The sleeves of her red blouse were too short, the tank top she wore over top of it too green. I snuck a glance at the lower half: burgundy jeans and pale-brown shoes. The *Fraggle Rock* look, I guess. I hoped it wasn't contagious.

"I don't see a problem with your qualifications. They're a bit dated, but we do in-service training any-way, so we can make it work... I have a few other inter-views before noon and some background checks to do, for security reasons."

"Of course."

"But I need the help ASAP, so things will move quickly. You'll hear by tomorrow."

"Great, I'll wait by the phone."

"You don't have a cell?"

"Yes, of course. Just a manner of speaking."

I had managed more than forty years without a cellphone. Some adjustments take time to develop.

The young woman who walked in after me had blue hair and countless rings through her lips, nose, eyebrows, and—believe it or not—earlobes. So many rings in which a small person's finger could get caught. I took out my cellphone, the sort that screams "technologically backward old fart" (Antoine can't imagine how anyone can be fully functional without the latest iPhone X24; with my antique 6, I'm four times as backwards), and texted Claudine.

> Guess who works at
> the school!

I don't have
time for this, spill!

> Guy!!!

Guy who?

> The carpenter!!!

What carpenter?

> The one who was working
> down the street from my

old place and brought
us to the hospital when
you broke your arm!

What's he doing
in an elementary school?

Secretary.

ARE YOU JOKING???

I know, I know. When you text, you're not supposed to use complete words or shout IN CAPS or put exclamation points everywhere. But Claudine and I don't give a crap about "today's" rules, whether for texting or a whole bunch of other things. We even go so far as to use capitals at the *beginning* of sentences and apostrophes for every contraction. Crazy, right? We tell anyone who'll listen that we're anarchists. Our children, almost lovingly, say "Nah, they're just old."

Of course.
He's carpentering.

Makeout potential
right there!!!

One: I don't even have
the job yet. Two: I doubt
he's single.

One: you'll get it. Two:
remember — we're

talking about kissing,
not having sex.

                                          You know how I feel
                                               about that.


We agreed to meet up later that evening over a glass of temporary solution. Ever since the trip to my house had been shortened to a flight of stairs, Claudine would often come up to seek refuge. Seeing as Adèle, likely foaming from every orifice, had just earned herself a second day of forced labour under her grandmother's watchful eye, my friend was in no rush to go home.

# 4

## In which I have a nice chat with Jacques and jump in feet first

On my way home, I stopped at the hardware store to pick up a garden gnome I'd ordered at the beginning of summer. It was a special model with a lantern that lit up, cute enough to prompt *Oh!*s of admiration from the most indifferent passerby. My gnome would wage a merciless war, meted out by AAA batteries, against my dark yard. Simon, the little neighbourhood kid who was crazy about my gnome village, would be tickled pink. I checked my email and the ringer on my phone for the thirtieth time. Radio silence. Blue Hair might be competition after all.

After that, I walked to the pharmacy to wander the aisles in search of new needs to meet (how would I know the new Vileda Bath Magic Hexagonal Cleaning Mop was guaranteed to change my life if I hadn't seen it yet?).

"Diane!"

I'd taken the turn with such assurance that it was impossible to change directions without looking like I was running away. To regain my composure, and so he wouldn't think I'd only come to pass the time, I threw a hurried glance at my phone. I was on the verge of working again; soon I wouldn't have a minute to myself.

"Ah...Jacques."

"Diane! What a coincidence!"

"I live right down the street."

"Oh yes, that's right..."

He wiped his face with one hand.

"I had a meeting in the area with some clients...3rd Street has really cleaned up!"

"Yeah, it's great."

"Tons of restaurants and little boutiques..."

Ever since Someone Else, Jacques had started wearing suits in impossible-to-name hues with matching accessories. *Co-ordinated* was the best word to describe his outfits. And as is often the case when we try a little too hard to be fashionable, the result was somewhere between refined elegance and tackiness. It depended on the angle. But from the back, it worked.

"Yeah, tons."

"You look good, Diane."

"Thanks."

"Did you lose weight?"

"Are you saying I look good *because* I look like I lost weight, or I look good *and* I look like I lost weight?"

I'd long stopped trying to come across as sane. The year before, I'd attacked his whore with a pitcher of water and demolished part of our old house with a sledgehammer. Among other things.

"Uh…"

"No, I haven't lost weight."

"Looks like it."

"You're buying formula?"

The whore's fake boobs might have been complicating things. The mean part of me smiled on the inside.

"It's for Terrence."

"That's right, I forgot. Like the manga *Candy Candy!*"

"Still happy with your duplex?"

"Oh my God, yes!"

"We could grab a bite together one of these days, what do you say?"

"I don't think so."

"Diane…"

"We're on good terms, let's keep it that way."

"The kids are really having a tough time."

"No, I don't think they are. You're the one having a tough time. You want me and your tramp to be buddy-buddy so you can sit back with a clear conscience and enjoy your midlife crisis."

"He's still their brother."

"For the moment," I said, "Terrence sleeps, eats, and shits formula all day long and doesn't give a rat's ass about his half-siblings—who, incidentally, are old enough to be parents themselves, in case you haven't noticed. At your age, men become grandfathers, not fathers."

"Diane, you need to move on, you're not the only one suffering here... You have to start over again, too..."

*Start over again!* Diving into freezing water would have been a thousand times less painful. Jacques's mouth continued moving, but I couldn't hear a thing. The vibrations from my phone reanimated my hand and I glanced at the screen instinctively: Charlotte wanted to know how the World's Best Mommy's interview had gone—and had added some cat emojis. Her text could not have come at a better time, cutting through the darkness that threatened to spread and give me the air of a punctured octopus. But like a half-dead superhero brought back to life by his enemy's vitriolic words ("Your father sobbed like a baby when I killed him, you miserable wretch!"), I found the strength to offer my periwinkle-clad ex-husband an amplified version of the radiant Diane I was capable of being. I decided to apply the positive-projection techniques my therapist had taught me, exceeding the prescribed limits as a return on my investment.

"Jacques..." (I took a deep breath, *Relax, Diane, relax*) "...I have incredible friends, a home I love, a rewarding job, a new boyfriend." (He flinched ever so slightly, and so did I). "I've never felt so good, so beautiful; the kids are happy and healthy, they're all in love. If I came face to face with God, I wouldn't even know what to ask for. The only one who hasn't moved on is you, old man."

His head recoiled slightly, his mouth and eyes wide open. At the last moment, he tightened his grip on the container of formula to keep it from slipping out of his hands. I kept going, taking full advantage of my epiphany.

"I'm your past, Charlene's your present. We belong to parallel universes that aren't meant to collide, so I don't know why you keep insisting they should. I'm happy without you, and you'll just have to accept that. Say hi to Charlene for me, okay?"

I stepped around him and let him watch me as I continued down the aisle without looking back. It was a good thing I'd dressed for the interview; it offered up an image of me that matched my lie and not the idle, embittered old woman he imagined me to be. Physically, anyway, and from the back.

I floated on my cloud of self-possession all the way up the back alley to the duplex, where I met with an unbelievable scene: Adèle, dressed in what amounted to a box of half-torn Kleenex, was beating a dusty rug hanging over the patio railing. The image was right out of a Marcel Pagnol film, only she was going at it with a grill spatula instead of a rattan carpet swatter. The moment she saw me, she began coughing histrionically, writhing as if in pain. I felt sorry, but not for her.

"Hello, Adèle! Doing a big clean?"

"Yeah, right, *cough cough...*"

"Your mother will be happy!"

Just then Claudine's mother appeared, carrying a laundry basket that was spilling over with darks. At eighty-four, her vigour surpassed that of her grand-daughter, whose muscles had never been required for anything more taxing than gym class.

"Hello, Mrs. Poulin!"

"Well now, if it isn't the lovely Diane!"

"Isn't that basket a little heavy for you?"

"Oh please, I don't feel a thing. You finally settled in upstairs?"

Rosanne was all there, with a resolve that was indomitable and a memory as sharp as a digital scale. She still rose with the rooster to peel vegetables and start the bread. The fact that humanity was hurtling toward self-destruction had no effect on her at all. I could picture her standing tall in the middle of an apocalyptic flood, like the little white house that defied the historic Saguenay deluge.

"Come up and see the place when you've got a minute."

"Maybe around sundown, once I get through enough here."

"Hey, Gran, why can't we just clean the rug with the vacuum?"

"All the vacuum does is suck up the top layer of grime. It doesn't reach the stuff on the bottom, or the fleas."

"What fleas? We don't even have pets."

"When you're done with that..."

"How do I know when to stop? There's always more dust!"

"When it doesn't puff anymore."

"But it keeps puffing!"

"Hit harder. If you did it every now and then, it wouldn't take this long. Then hang up this load when you're done. Start with the big pieces, they dry slower."

I spent the rest of the afternoon checking my phone, going through every section of the newspaper, and reading the SAQ ads down to the last detail. Cat-in-the-box was curled up in a ball on the couch, sleeping. My running shoes were kicking around the entryway, well behaved as always. The love story the sales clerk at the sporting goods store hoped for us had been doomed from the start: my aversion to physical suffering has always been stronger than my desire to lose weight or live to old age. The run-walk approach had quickly given way to just walking, which was more my pace. Buried in my soft flesh, my shrivelled heart would give out in some predictable scenario of my own doing. At times, to stop feeling so guilty, I would pounce on reports or articles warning against the dangers of overtraining as if they were aimed at me. I even congratulated myself for having dodged the thousand perils that pave the runner's world.

I was in front of the mirror examining my neck wrinkles when Claudine arrived with an emergency rosé.

"Knock, knock! Anybody home?"

I walked over to her, holding back the skin of my neck with both hands to mimic the effect of surgery.

"Look, like this."

"Like this what?"

"They'd just have to take a piece from each side, like this, and sew it up in the back. Nobody would even know."

"You want to make yourself look younger for the hot carpenter, eh?"

"That has nothing to do with it."

"What about your face? You'll need to do something there, or the whole thing'll clash."

"Yeah..."

"And once the top's done, you'll have to do the

bottom so it fits, too. The chest wrinkles, the that's-its jiggling under your arms, your stomach, your leg fat..."

"Okay, fine. What're we drinking?"

"Pink, my pretty, like the movie. And if you don't get the job, we'll find something to renovate in the house."

I told her about my interview with Andrée and every word of my run-in with Jacques.

"She can't breastfeed with those huge plastic tits?"

"Or she needs her beauty sleep at night. They might have a nanny, which would explain the formula."

"You told him, the old fucker! Hah! In your face! Go start over yourself!"

We were still on our first glass when Rosanne showed up with a big boiling pot resting on an oven mitt. Not the least bit winded.

"Ma! You'll hurt yourself with that! You should've told me!"

"Oh, stop! The day I can't pick up a pot of soup is the day I want you to put me in the ground."

"What kind of soup?"

"Leftovers. I cleaned out your fridge."

"Ma, you're supposed to be resting."

"I'll rest when I'm dead. It was a real mess in there, I couldn't find the margarine."

"We only have butter. You should've asked Adèle to clean out the fridge. You're here to supervise, not work."

"That poor child! She's all thumbs. I feel sorry for

her, the way you've spoiled her. Can't even change a roll of toilet paper!"

"Would you like a glass of rosé, Mrs. Poulin?"

"'Atta girl, it can't hurt! You mixed up the rest of the white and the red?"

"No, no, it comes like this."

"Then they mix it at the store first, or they put a helluva lot of water in the red. Lemme give it a try, I'll let you know…"

I'd just served us each a bowl of soup when the Shitmans appeared, holding their ritual king cans and sauntering over to the old, broken-down car seats that lined the alley. They were light years from the nocturnal couple that had been my neighbours for the last decade of my former life, retirees glued to their windows. These guys parked themselves in the same spot almost every night, save when it rained, shouting a stream of nonsense back and forth that comprised no more than about twenty words from the dictionary. Although the wind often blew their voices as far as our balconies, we could never make out what exactly they were discussing.

"Shit, man … the guy showed up … shit, you wouldn't believe it, man … with all his shit, man … what a little fucker…"

"The same fucking guy?"

"Yeah, man! The other one, too, man, a real fucking idiot…"

"Shit, man, are you kidding me?"

"SHIT, MAN! NO WAY! THE SAME FUCKING THING, MAN!"

As we were listening distractedly to the muddle of swearing and snatches of incoherent conversation, Adèle managed to drag herself up to our perch.

"Wow, you're living the life, eh? I'm all by myself down there working my ass off while you're up here taking it easy. Awesome, guys..."

"Hello, sweeeeetie!"

"Seriously, don't ask me to be your maid tomorrow. I'm not a servant, I have rights."

"And responsibilities, darling."

"You can't lock me up and make me work like a slave! Plus, I'm a minor, it's in the Charter of Rights and Freedoms. I won't have it!"

We'd never seen Adèle apply such intensity to anything she did or said in her whole life. Instead of telling her mother off, as she typically did when she was angry (we'd expected something more along the lines of "You can shove your responsibilities up your ass!"), she was defending her position with an argument based in civil law. Amazing. Unfortunately for her, Rosanne was quick with a comeback, and after a few sips of rosé, she was almost waxing poetic.

"Bring me your Charter, I'll stuff it up my cabbage roll!"

Claudine burst out laughing, spitting wine everywhere. With a little muscular acrobatics, I managed to swallow the sip I'd just taken. Adèle had already disappeared downstairs by the time we caught our breath. The sound of the door slamming ricocheted over to the Shitmans, who briefly suspended their philosophizing so they wouldn't miss out on a fight. Mrs. Poulin didn't seem impressed.

"Someone sure coulda used a few good kicks in the ass."

"Don't start, Ma..."

The sun was setting when I received the long-awaited call. I hurried inside so I could be alone to let the first seconds of emotion, whatever it would be, sink in. Andrée asked if I could come in at 6:30 the next morning. Three shifts a day, morning-noon-night, separated by breaks, like a pie.

"I GOT THE JOB! I GOT THE JOB!"

"I knew you would! You're on fire, old lady!"

Claudine made the sign of the devil's horns with each hand.

"Shit, man, you're on fire, man!"

"I'm going to work tomorrow...that's so weird..."

"Let's go celebrate! Everyone over to La Casserole!"

"Come down and eat instead, I made a big pot of spaghetti sauce."

"We'll freeze it, Ma, don't worry. Nothing will go to

waste. Come with us, you're gonna love their cassoulet."

"Lord, can't you two drink and eat a simple meal like the rest of the world? I don't see why it always has to be such a fuss."

"It's white beans with a ton of meat. You'll love it."

"Well, you can't go wrong with beans if you know how to cook 'em. Do they have some of the pink stuff over there?"

"You wash it down with red, no choice."

Adèle didn't deign to come. Too vegetarian, and too busy brooding over the agonies of slave life, she was flopped on her canopy bed, TV remote in one hand and an $8.50 Organic Tutti Vio smoothie — paid for by her cruel mother, of course — in the other. The local greengrocer had found a way to sell his leftover produce: put it through the blender and mark it up, using flashy names to disguise its lack of appeal and freshness.

Later that night, after I'd returned home, unconscionably inebriated for an old woman on the eve of her first day back at work, I took off my socks and felt my heels. The skin was softer, the cracks had healed enough to keep the blood on the inside. I was ready to jump in, feet first.

# 5

## In which I turn into a princess

What I would learn by working in a school was something I had already been taught by Jacinthe, my charming ex-sister-in-law, who for years had foisted her two little monsters on me every Wednesday despite lacking an invitation to do so: the problem with kids is often their parents.

I was in the midst of greeting the third student who was part of what would officially become "my" group when Andrée threw me into the clutches of a worried mother desperate to speak to whoever was in charge.

"Are you the new aide?"

"Yes, hi, I'm Diane. Today is my first day. Delighted to meet you!"

The naïve candour was a bad idea. Parents of little

kids — kindergarteners, five-ish years old, mid-thigh height — don't like leaving their blessed progeny to first-day-on the-jobbers. They prefer stability, experience acquired over time, expertise that's been proven. Basically, they want us to cut our teeth on someone else's children. Which is understandable. There's nothing reassuring about a youngish old lady with bloodshot eyes appearing out of nowhere on the third week of September. The poor mother's jaw, relaxed for a fraction of a second by chagrin, managed to freeze into a fake smile that hinted at a well-practised professional.

"So you're in charge of the group for the rest of the year?"

"If all goes well, yes."

"There's been a new aide almost every day for three weeks now, it's psychologically damaging to the children. Célyane's been totally thrown off."

"I can understand, ma'am. We're working to fix the problem, given the context."

"Well. I wanted to speak to you because Célyane doesn't feel so well today. Oh, and by the way, it's with a y."

When I heard the name without this distinction, I'd pictured CELI-Anne, as in *Compte-d'épargne-libre-d'impôt*-Anne. Tax-Free-Savings-Account Anne. Some creative spellings work better than others.

"What seems to be the problem?"

"She has a stomach ache."

"Any diarrhea or vomiting?"

"No, no, no, just a regular stomach ache. Like everyone else."

Everyone had a stomach ache? This was the first I'd heard of it. My hand instinctively moved to the little bulge below my own waist.

"Okay."

"She just needs to take it easy."

"Wouldn't it be better to take it easy at home?"

"No, no, no! It's important that she's with friends."

"Except if she's sick..."

"Well anyway, I wrote her a note. Here."

"A note for...?"

"Miss Sophie."

"Ah..."

"Célyane's teacher."

"Oh yes, of course. Sorry."

"So she can be exempt from doing certain activities if she doesn't feel up to it."

"Activities like what?"

"Phys. ed., for instance. It might be better if she sat that out, so she doesn't make it worse."

"Make what worse?"

"Her stomach ache."

"It might help if she moved around a bit..."

"It doesn't work like that with Célyane."

Maybe there'd been some genetic mutations since I'd sent my kids to school. Charlotte was right: I would have to keep an open mind.

"Running makes it hurt more."

"Doesn't that worry you?"

"No, no, no."

"Have you taken her to see a doctor?"

She gave me a stern look, her smile tight. The kind of woman who could break a few skulls, if need be.

"Of course."

The whole thing reeked of bullshit, but I couldn't see any way to call her on the baloney without pissing her off. I was familiar with the tune, though. From kindergarten and all the way through college, my son Antoine had put his imagination into high gear inventing ailments to get out of phys. ed. — from a pathological fear of balls to brain cancer, no less. Yet I'd never gone along with the lies, always more outraged by them than anyone. Nonetheless, I reminded myself that I didn't even have an hour of seniority under my belt and trouble could wait a bit. Plus, Andrée had given me a subtle warning just before the kids arrived, a friendly whisper full of implication: "Go into it thinking the parents are clients who are always right, and you'll be fine." A child's education and a fish's freshness, same difference.

"Okay, I'll make sure the teacher receives the note. Don't you worry."

"Thank you."

"I imagine that if the stomach ache gets worse, even without taking phys. ed., we should let you know?"

Throughout our conversation I could see a boy named Devan, out of the corner of my right eye, violently smashing a doll's head against the ground. Was he trying to make it explode? It didn't appear he'd been taught the difference between a toy to be coddled and a hammer. Unfazed, the big pitcher of Kool-Aid Ice Cool on his T-shirt continued to smile — puns often do live up to the product advertised. Andrée intervened just as the toy's stitching gave way. Chucky's head went flying into the bookcase over in the quiet area, eyes rolling.

"I don't think it'll come to that, it's just an ordinary stomach ache. Like I said, she'll be fine if she takes it easy. Besides, I might be hard to get ahold of today."

Another pro's smile in faux plastic. This time she gritted her teeth ever so slightly. I nodded, Japanese-style, and was relieved when she seemed satisfied. She blinked, spun around, then took off on her four-inch heels.

The last fifteen kids spilled in, one after the other, some with oversized backpacks and milk moustaches, others with a pressing urge to pee, their eyes puffy from tears and sleep, their confused and desperate eagerness to be big kids while remaining little ones, their need to express themselves at the mercy of their churning brains. They didn't know me, but all of them wanted to tell me what they'd brought for lunch; to talk about their cat; to show me their new teeth, their scribbled artwork, their light-up shoes, their *Frozen* Band-Aids. They couldn't help running and jumping everywhere, especially on the bean bag in the reading corner, which, an hour later, I wanted to hurl out the window. They were always wanting someone else's game or book, and all of them talked at the same time — shouting, of course, to get my attention. In short, they were fabulously alive, and I couldn't begrudge them that; nothing is more exhausting than a slug of a kid who needs, in addition to everything else, someone to breathe life into them. The chaos was therefore reassuring. In the end, these children might not be so different from the ones I'd known in the previous millennium.

Some students, like quiet little Pavel, with his pale blue eyes, stood out from the rest. He acted the same as most of the others, smiling and having fun, but not a sound escaped his lips. Physically, the doctors had been clear, everything was functional. But as francization courses hadn't succeeded in prying out the slightest syllable from him, the administration had decided that integrating him into a regular class would help him to "defrost" — to conquer, through doses of normality, the knot that had formed in his mouth. And since we had no idea what else to do, we waited. Andrée gave me a quick rundown of things to get me up to speed as, over in her corner and transparent as the breeze, Julia endlessly counted a stack of cards she gripped in her little hands.

"Her mother wants us to let her be."

"What are on the cards?"

"Unicorns, marshmallow men, all sorts of things. I don't think it matters, she doesn't look at them. All she does is count them."

"All the time?"

"Every time there's a new rule or we change rooms or activities. It's like a password; if she doesn't count them, she won't move. Once she's done, she can function again."

"Is there a diagnosis?"

"Nervous tic."

"Oh, come on..."

"Talk to Sophie about it."

In addition to learning each of my charges' idiosyncrasies, I would need to familiarize myself with the rest: schedules, school rules, each activity's specific routine, the accident reports to be completed and filed, the mechanics of room changes, the different classroom materials and where they were stored, the thousand and one nuances of the relationships governing the school's organizations, as well as those included in my contract, which was to be renewed every three months (which suited me just fine, all things considered—if I couldn't handle the job, I had a formal exit strategy). Here and there, Andrée dropped the names of the teachers and other aides—all of them women—whom she discreetly pointed out to me in the hallways and in the schoolyard so that I knew what to expect. I didn't retain much other than to avoid Miss Kathleen, a bitch of Olympic proportions who cracked the whip in grade 6B and spat venom haphazardly from the bits of gossip she caught and threw like bombs. She was an ageless woman with an acerbity that could pollute even the most fragrant of atmospheres.

When Miss Sophie showed up, with all the weight of her twenty-seven-and-a-half years (I couldn't help asking), her mermaid hair and tanned glow, I suddenly felt very old. By some failure of the imagination, I'd thought Miss Sophie would match the archaic vision I had kept, despite myself, of a schoolmistress with a cardigan and a tight bun. I handed her Célyane's mother's note. She glanced at the name, then lowered her eyes and sighed, a barely audible "Again" escaping her lips. Mid-September was feeling like November. At this rate, she would ride into the half-century burnout well before her fifties.

I came home for a rejuvenating nap before attacking the lunch hour. There were definite advantages to living a short walk from the school. Cat-in-the-box was waiting for me on the doorstep, an earthworm the size of a garter snake in his mouth. At a different time in my life, I would have received flowers. When you start over, you take what gifts you can get.

As expected, lunchtime gave me countless opportunities to be imaginative, resourceful, and patient as never before. Some kids couldn't recognize their lunch boxes, others had lost theirs; the microscopic Éléonore started screaming like a banshee when she noticed cheese in her sandwich, Loïc stuck three raisins up his nose (which I had to fish out with my eyebrow tweezers), Tarek began spitting on the floor and clawing at his tongue when he bit into an onion (?!?) the size of an apple, Léah and Fauvèle (?!?) made a huge fuss about eating with Louane ("Her lunch stinks!"), Coralie cried because she was still hungry after downing her pint-sized tuna wrap ("You can have my sandwich, sweetie..."), and Devan...Devan made art by jumping with both feet onto his juice box. There for emergencies, the horrible brown paper was unable to absorb even the smallest mess. One of the mothers had left instructions for reheating her child's meal: *Microwave uncovered for 1:30 (90 seconds). Cut the pasta into bite-sized pieces, mixing in the sauce. Leave whatever is leftover inside the container so I can see how much he ate. Do not give him the chocolate pudding unless he eats at least half the pasta. Encourage him to eat some fruit. Thank you. Laure (Laurent's mom*). In the time it took to show the note to Andrée, Laurent had gulped down the pudding—though he'd smeared a good deal of it across the right side of his face, which we had to wipe with the brown paper, poor kid. He didn't touch the pasta.

"This happens sometimes at the beginning of the year with first-borns. I'll put his name on the list of parents we'll try to flag down this afternoon."

"What do we tell them?"

"Sandwich, or Thermos for hot meals with the food already cut up. And just as it says on the eighteen copies of the rules we sent everyone, the only desserts allowed are fruit, cheese, and yogurt. No peanuts, no nuts, no sesame, nothing else— not ever, not in any form or for any reason. We'll also put Lucka's parents on the list."

"For...?"

"Can't you hear him?"

She cupped her ear, swivelling her head toward the bathroom area set up at the back of the classroom. Over the cacophony of little voices that were laughing, shouting, and whining came the persistent wail of syllables on repeat.

"I'm done! I said, *I'm done*! I'M DONE! I'M DOOONE!"

"No!"

"No is correct. Kids in kindergarten are expected to wipe themselves. So we'll talk to the parents."

"We should add Devan's parents to the list, I imagine?"

"Good idea. And you know what? I'll give you the pleasure of talking to them."

"But today's my first day with him."

"All his days have been the same so far."

"But they won't believe me, I'm new."

"Don't tell them that."

"Why do I get the feeling you know them?"

"Because you're a smart girl."

The use of the word *girl* was generous; she also had an accordion of wrinkles around her mouth when she smiled. But they were softer, darker, prettier wrinkles. White skin doesn't age as well.

"He has a brother in grade 2."

"Oh! Let me guess: *We Need to Talk About Kevin*."

"You're close—Jason."

"*Friday the 13th!* My God . . ."

"Five bucks says you can't guess how the dad will explain away his little angel's behaviour."

"ADHD?"

"Nah, that would actually make sense."

After leaving Miss Sophie to her classroom, I headed over to the grade 5 and 6 wing, the one that was being renovated. I reached into my bag for the ice pack and came across my cellphone: "Don't forget, happy hour at Igloo. Come over as soon as you're done. I'll be there early. Eye on the prize: trading tongues. Claud xx." Like I could show up in athleisure, no makeup, no heels. Jim walked past me at that moment, straining under the weight of what appeared to be a huge roll of electrical wire over one shoulder. Even through his shirt, his muscles outlined gentle peaks and valleys. His hard hat, half covering his eyes, gave him an untamed sort of look. Although the "slow motion" function is available on just about every device, it doesn't exist in real life — a most regrettable oversight in technological evolution.

"Hello, Jim!"

"Ah! Hi, Diane!"

I was touched that he'd remembered my name.

"I'm bringing back your ice pack. The little guy ended up keeping it for a while."

"How's he doing?"

"He'll be fine."

"Sorry, but I have to take this up to the boys."

"I'll put it in your cooler. Is Guy around?"

"On the scaffolding, west side."

"Thanks."

It took me a while to pick him out of the crew of men carting around the metal supports and huge wood planks they would turn into elevated sidewalks for the impending megastructure. The portion of the wall they were working on was fenced off, of course, and

I couldn't get too near. What with the construction that was being done just steps away from the school-yard, they needed to make sure the area was secure at all costs. It would be impossible to run into him "by chance" and exchange some small talk. I was just about to turn around when I heard a loud "Hey!"

"Diane!"

It was him, or at least his waving arm. He walked toward me with brio, propelled by the graceful force of his powerful strides. Hormones have a fascinating way of bedazzling what would otherwise be bafflingly ordinary. And despite the death of my reproductive system foretold, mine had just set off a feedback loop that jeopardized my physical and mental stability. As proof, I had my fingers hooked through a link of the safety fence, my stomach was in knots, and my cheeks were flushed as I watched a man built like a prosper-ous farmer walk toward me as his colleagues whistled teasingly. I wanted to film the scene for Claudine. The dull calm that dominated my life only a day earlier had been put through a defibrillator. Thank you, doctor.

"Hey, hey! How's it going? Were you looking for me?"

"I was just coming to say hi."

"That's nice of you."

"I'm working as a teacher's aide, I have part of the afternoon off."

With one hand gripping the fence, Guy flashed a beautiful set of teeth. I swallowed as best as I could. I had to come up with something interesting to move the conversation in a desirable direction.

"Are you doing the brick, too?"

"No, we're on the windows now."

"What a job . . ."

"The older window systems are tougher to dismantle."

"I bet."

Bravo, great direction, Diane.

"I was wondering . . ."

I had no idea what I was planning to say, skydiving without a parachute.

"I was wondering whether . . ."

"BOSS?"

Guy's head whipped around like a broken spring.

"THE DELIVERY'S HERE! THE TRAILER'S OUT FRONT!"

"'Scuse me, I gotta run, my wood's here."

"Go, go. We'll talk later."

He dashed off, shouting orders as he ran. He wouldn't have been moving any faster if someone had died. Once I arrived at the front of the building, I understood the urgency: two rigs the size of ocean liners were completely blocking the street. The drivers brought to a halt behind them were already losing patience, saturating the air with their habitual (and unproductive) symphony of honks. The man behind the wheel of a fire-engine-red Honda Civic with a rear spoiler was leaning halfway out the window, swearing loudly at the convoy that idled motionless before him.

"You bunch of morons! Move outta the way! You're holding us all hostage, goddamn jackasses! You shoulda barred the street off at the corner, not right in the middle of the block! I doubt you even have permits, you bunch of fuckin' rookies!"

"HEY!" I yelled. "RELAX!"

It came out all on its own, like a surprise burp. Evidently, the defibrillator had roused all sorts of monsters in me.

"Yelling won't make them go any faster!"

"What's it to you, lady?"

"You're in front of a school, there are kids at every window!"

"THEN THEY SHOULD MOVE!"

"CAN'T YOU SEE THEY'RE UNLOADING WOOD?"

"THEY SHOULDN'T BE BLOCKING THE STREET!"

"DOESN'T YOUR CAR HAVE REVERSE, YOU DAMN FOOL? I BET YOU DON'T EVEN HAVE A LICENCE!"

"GET LOST, YOU CRAZY OLD BAT! I SHOULDN'T HAVE TO BACK UP!"

I was, in a word, unhinged. My foot went flying, of its own accord, into the driver's side door. I could have done better with a sledgehammer.

"Ah, FUCK!"

He got out of the car wielding a crowbar. Early thirties, sharp features, a wild look in his eye. A real asshole whose hot rod had tinted windows and oversized wheels. He dangled the tool like someone about to wind up. Just then two workers appeared, their fists clenched, followed by Guy, who was all smiles.

"Hey, bro! I think you should get back in your car."

"The goddamn bitch just kicked it!"

"The car's fine. Get the hell outta here."

"Shit, man, I'm gonna fuck you up..."

"You have a weapon and you're making threats in front of lots of witnesses and lots of phones, bro. I hope you're cool with the police."

He blanched slightly. The other construction workers approached slowly, like in a number from *West Side Story*. Something about the sound of the word *police* had put a chip in his arrogance. He gritted his teeth and flipped the middle finger of his free hand.

"I'd ask you to apologize to the lady, but I can see you're in a hurry."

He sucked in air through his nose and cleared his throat, hocking up all his rage at our feet in a juicy, gelatinous blob.

"I think you've got a problem with manners in general, bro."

Once he was back at the wheel, he flipped us the finger again before muttering a string of four-letter words, twisting his neck as he reversed. One of the workers, a little rosy-cheeked wonder, pinched the tip of his hard hat and nodded in my direction. Guy walked over.

"That was some kick!"

"Couldn't help it, I just wanted to fly at him. You're so calm—how do you do it?"

"No use getting mad at a dick like that."

He smiled up at me, like a model from a Sears catalogue. He'd seen his fair share of dicks—that you could tell from his quiet display of strength and the authority in his voice.

"I better get back. Thanks again, Lady Di."

Once again he put a furtive hand on my arm. If it were a movie I'd have jumped on him and we'd have French kissed as some super-famous song arranged for ukulele played in the background. In real life, I did what I could. I whipped out my phone as soon as there were a few metres between us.

"You'll never believe this."

"You already lost your job?"

"I almost got into a fight!"

"A fight? Who with?"

"Some dick, it doesn't matter. But guess who stood up for me?"

"Don't you work in a kindergarten class?"

"Guess!"

"The janitor."

"No, someone we know!"

"Céline Dion!"

"No, stupid . . . *Guy*! The carpenter!"

"You almost got into a fight with a dick and Guy stood up for you? Big day at the office!"

"And wait for this—guess what he called me? Lady Di!"

"Ah hah."

"Come on! *Lady Di*!"

"Lady Di was a princess who ended up smashing into a wall."

"And how old was she when she died? Thirty-six candles in the wind. What do you call that?"

"Dying young."

"It's called a whole lot of compliments in three syllables."

"Or the art of deluding yourself in three syllables."

"I've gotta go, I have an appointment with Sabrina."

"You're getting your hair blown out for J.P.?"

"What do you mean, for J.P.?"

"Happy hour!"

"Shit! I totally forgot!"

I looked down at my canvas loafers streaked with raspberry applesauce. Or tomato sauce. Or both.

"The grey looked good on you, it really worked with your natural colour."

"It makes me look old. I'm not as ready as I thought."

"It's really in, even young girls are dyeing their hair grey!"

"That's just it, I'm not young."

"The fifties of today are the thirties of our parents' generation."

"Grandparents'."

"You know what I mean."

"Somebody called me a crazy old bat today."

The three other clients, waiting their turn in chairs and at the sink, turned our way. Hair appointments are always so intimate.

"Who said that? Some idiot?"

"Yeah, but still. I'm not even fifty."

Sabrina swivelled my chair to face her so that we could talk eye to eye.

"Okay. What's going on?"

"It's not that time of the month, don't worry."

"If you're going to ruin more than a year of my work by colouring on top of it, you need to tell me what's up."

"I just feel like a change."

"It's never just about a change, there's always some-thing else going on—we talked about this."

I gave her a goofy smile.

"Okay. Positive vibes, I like it. What did you have in mind?"

"Dark blond."

"Dark blond? Like who?"

"What do you mean, like who?"

"There has to be a reason, or at least a source of inspiration."

To dodge her fearsome insight, I made a mental list of all my acquaintances—old and new.

"I have this colleague at school..."

"Uh-huh..."

"She has really pretty hair... thick like mine, but a dark blond. Brown with blond highlights, actually..."

"And whose hair would you say it looks like?"

"What do you mean?"

"Do you have a picture of this colleague?"

"Well, no, I only just started working there..."

"Then to get an idea of the colour we need to go online and find a picture of someone famous."

"Well...uh, let me think...hmm...maybe... yeah..."

"Okay then, who?"

"Lady Di?"

"Oh boy! You want Lady Di's hair?"

"I'm talking about the colour, not the cut."

"I should hope so! But even for the colour, your colleague's a little behind the times ..."

She winked at me. You can't fool Sabrina. Therapists and hairdressers should team up and offer their services in adjoining spaces, like doctors and pharmacists.

"You'll have to come back, there's not enough time left today."

"What do you mean?"

"It'll take a good three hours. I'll have to bleach your hair twice, otherwise you'll end up with a piss-yellow blond you're going to hate for a long, long time. You want to look like Cyndi Lauper?"

"*Nooo.*"

I returned to school well before the end of classes, since Andrée still had lots to show me. Miss Sophie had taken her aside during recess to discuss the intervention plan she wanted to develop for Devan. She'd had enough of him swimming breaststroke on a table while the other students tried to work—meaning cutting, pasting, and drawing. If she were able to get all the support staff on board, there was a better chance his parents might co-operate. To hear the staff talk, I could tell that managing this would be no small feat.

During the end-of-day chaos, I would have to learn

to divide my attention in a million different directions against the backdrop of students' names being endlessly repeated through the walkie-talkies' snowy buzz. I'd need two or three extra arms, nimbler legs, bionic eyes. When Devan's name sounded over the sleet of the waves, I was consoling little Léah, who'd "scaped" her knee, keeping an eye on a surreal form of soccer—the kids were running with the ball in their hands—and reprimanding the grade 5 boys for not letting Éléonore line up for pear ball. Andrée gave me a thumbs-up, signalling she would take over, and grabbed her transceiver with the other hand.

"Sylvie, could you ask whoever comes for Devan to meet us at the back door? We need to speak to mom or dad."

"Roger that, I'm sending dad over."

I headed to the door at the far end of the schoolyard. A man in a charcoal suit, with his head held high and bangs like David Beckham, placed one beautifully shod foot onto the asphalt, rubbing his hands together. I figured he didn't belong to Devan—eye colour, mostly—but I played dumb just so I could hear his voice.

"Hello! Are you Devan's father?"

"Hello! No, I'm Éléonore's."

One of *my* dads, cool.

"Oh! It's a pleasure to meet you. My name is Diane, I'm Éléonore's new teacher's aide."

"Ah! Nice to meet you, miss."

"She's with the rest of the group, over in the back."

"How did it go today?"

"It was a good day, quite good. She's crying a bit now, but that's just because of the pear ball."

"Oh right! She told me about that, the pear game."

"You've never heard of pear ball?"

"No."

"It's the game you see over there, the metal pole with the swinging ball shaped like a . . . pear."

Andrée called it cock ball. I tried really hard not to think about it. Back when I was in school, it was prison ball, a kind of punching bag that was mandatory for everyone. The concept of free play was a little more restrictive then and there wasn't a square inch of asphalt where you could pass the time alone. No trees or play structures or urban-chic benches carved from local wood on which to comfortably chill. But I could see why they had done away with prison ball, in many ways a cruel game that reproduces the most fundamental laws of nature prevailing in the wild and in the business world. In fact, I'm not really sure which—prison ball or savage capitalism—inspired the other.

"The kids stand facing each other and take turns hitting the pear ball with two hands. You lose your turn when you miss it, and then the next person in line gets a turn. It moves along pretty quickly."

"Ah! Okay."

"But Éléonore is too short, she'd have to stand on tiptoe and even then..."

"Can't you lower the pole? Or the ball?"

"The posts are set in concrete foundations and the ball straps aren't very long. There might be other kinds of balls, I'm not sure...but it's not fun for the little kids, I know."

He frowned, bringing his fists to his hips. Nice shirt, slim waist, no belly, bravo.

"Hmm...can I take a closer look?"

"Sure, go ahead."

"Thanks, and have a nice day."

"You too!"

Just behind him, in a hoodie flecked with paint and his hair a dishevelled mess, a man was walking toward me, chin up, looking menacing. Stuck behind one ear was either an unlit cigarette or a pencil, it was hard to say. He was fidgeting nervously. I approached him slowly, so as not to startle him.

"Hello! Are you Devan's father?"

"Yeah."

No handshake, no hello, head like a bird darting this way and that. I thought: wiring issue, coke, PTSD. I also thought: prejudice.

"My name is Diane, I'm the new aide for Miss Sophie's group."

"Okay."

"We had a bit of trouble with Devan today."

"Okay."

"He started off the day by breaking a doll."

"He doesn't like dolls."

"He was the one who picked it out."

"Okay."

"And he pushed another student during lunch. He hurt Loïc, and so we had to get involved. There's a note in his file, along with a message for you in his agenda. Maybe Devan will tell you about it."

"Okay."

"Then, while the kids were eating, he jumped onto his juice box with both feet and made it explode. There was juice everywhere. The floor is still sticky, even after we cleaned it. He needs to learn not to do that with juice ... or with food in general."

"Okay."

I'd thought his son's antics would prompt cries of indignation and excuses, at the very least a discussion, requests for clarification, exclamations. But no, he remained stone-faced as I listed his son's misdeeds, as if I were telling him a fable in Mandarin. Maybe it was just how he took in information. It was still early in the conversation, and I could give him the benefit of the doubt.

"It's also very difficult to get his attention during

group activities. He gets up without asking, doesn't follow directions..."

"It's not his fault."

"Oh?"

"It's because he's friggin' brilliant."

"Oh..."

"He's already doing Lego 14+. He even finished a Technic 16+ all by himself. I was the same when I was little, except the Technic sets didn't exist back then."

He opened his arms wide, turned his palms to the sky, and threw his head back, smiling. Boom!

"If he's that smart, he should be able to follow directions."

"He gets restless when he's bored."

"So does everyone. But that's no excuse for..."

"And when he's not stimulated, he makes trouble."

"And when he pushes other kids?"

"He was pushed first. He stands up for himself when he gets picked on. Did you ask him why he pushed the other kid?"

"It doesn't matter why, at school that kind of behaviour is unacceptable. We don't tolerate violence in any form, for any reason."

"Violence? Oh, come on, he didn't split the kid's head open..."

Collaboration would be difficult. Antagonism curled around his every remark and excuse. Listening to him rationalize his son's behaviour with a thousand and one defences that clearly held no water, I got the impression he'd end up sympathizing with poor Devan, who'd had to put up with us all day—us, the big dolts unable to adapt to his giftedness. I'd have gleefully smashed a trinket or two to calm down, maybe even a small piece of furniture. A chair, at the very least.

By the time I walked back to Andrée, she was making a superhuman effort to contain her laughter. I looked around and realized that the other aides were casting me sidelong glances as they tied a shoe here or broke up an argument there. The whole thing smacked of a conspiracy.

"Okay, I get it, that was my initiation. Everyone ganged up on me. It was all arranged."

"No way. *Pfff*...I swear! *Pfff*...What'd he say?"

"A load of shit."

"*Pfff*..."

Linda, one of the nice aides from grade 3, approached feigning a need to watch the kids around us. Over the jumble of Mathildes, Emmas, and Williams, our radio sets were spitting out syllables forming children's names that my ear was just beginning to decipher. "Kelloua in 2B, Laïla..." "Which Laïla?" "Laïla Grondin, and send over Soutek while you're at it, I see his dad. Philomia in 4C..."

"Hang on a sec, let's wait until he leaves...okay, tell us everything."

"Honestly, it worries me. That guy drives a car."

"Did he tell you why his son is a little monster?"

"Ish."

"Well?"

"Because the kid's too smart."

"*Whoaaa!*"

Andrée and Linda burst out laughing in unison, slapping their thighs. We must have looked like a beer commercial.

"I guess his brother has the same issue?"

They both nodded, unable to speak. If you're going to laugh, you might as well go all out.

"Did he tell you about the Legos?"

More nodding. The only sound was the hiss of air fighting its way back into their lungs.

"And with no building instructions, either..."

They were crying. I could tell we were going to get along just fine.

Andrée sent me home just before 6 p.m. There were only a few students left: the ones I would become used to seeing until the end of most days. The ones who preferred to keep on playing with their friends rather than go home and be bored. The ones whose parents were stuck at work or in traffic. And the ones whose parents, for all sorts of more-or-less legitimate reasons, wanted them to stay in the after-school care program for as long as possible. Which meant a whole lot of kids eating late dinners. By the time I arrived home, I was so tired and sweaty it felt like I'd taken up jogging again. Fortunately, the only living being requiring my attention could get by with a bit of dry kibble and a few pats on the head.

# 6

## In which Claudine drinks Negronis
## and opens her arms wide

I was still fragrant with soap when I arrived in front
of Igloo. The walls, surprise surprise, were made
of very '70s-looking glass cubes that stifled the light
filtering through. The young hostess was wearing a
dress the size of a pocket square that somehow covered all her important bits and was magically strung
together with something resembling dental floss.
She couldn't have weighed half as much as me. From
behind, only her rear end was covered. The arc of her
lower back stretched the fabric into a plunging curve
until it bloomed across the contour of her buns. She
was as naked as possible while still pretending to be
clothed. Her white arm—the underside of which was
impeccable—formed a straight line before my eyes,

her index finger pointing to the glass canopy beneath which a noisy crowd had gathered.

"If you're meeting people for a drink, they'll be over there, standing room only. We're running a special on cocktails until seven, and pints are five bucks. If you want a table to eat afterwards, you gotta give me your cell number."

"Oh? Why's that?"

"So I can call you when the table's ready."

"What if I don't have a cell?"

She opened her eyes extremely wide, as if I'd just told her the internet was about to explode. Her lower lip, which was oddly plump, went slack. It was clear my question had shaken her entire world view.

"Uh...I dunno..."

"It's fine, I'm only here for a drink."

I cut through the crowd with my out-of-touch middle-aged woman's smile. Half the people I bumped into were holding their phones. They must have been waiting for The Call.

Claudine, who had arrived early, as promised, was already in full cocktail mode. Around her, familiar faces chatted in small groups, hands gripping their drinks. (At fifteen bucks a pop, they'd do well to hang on tight). I gave some nods and a few polite hugs, settling for a gentle smile when I got to Josy-Josée. True to herself, she wore a too-tight pantsuit in an unlikely colour—olive with undertones of copper sulphate—and matching shoes. With time and distance, the animosity I'd once felt toward her had been extinguished, like a fire without oxygen. These people belonged to my former life; they'd continued to turn the pages of their calendars in a vortex that didn't include me. Thinking back to my office, perched in an overly air-conditioned glass tower with beige elevators; to the rigorously scheduled breaks, the flavourless coffee from automatic dispensers, the tedium of repetitive tasks, the tyranny of all-powerful bosses, and the pettiness of bored co-workers, my heart went out to these poor little awkward, messy, quibbling souls.

"Christ, you're late!"

"I had to wash up and change first. My arms were covered in paint and my pants in bodily fluids that weren't my own."

"Okay, you're grossing me out."

"Believe it or not, you'll get used to it."

"You didn't see Sabrina? Your hair doesn't look any different... Well now, if it isn't the dashing J.P., here to grace us with his presence!"

"Hey, hey! Look who's back!"

J.P. opened his arms to embrace me. Through some fortunate mechanism of interlocking bodies, my face wound up pressed against his neck—oh Lord, the smell!—and his lips were in my hair, practically touching my ear. Goosebumps ran from the lobe all the way down to the tip of my right toe.

"What're you drinking, J.P.?" asked Claudine. "And you, Lady Di? The server's coming over, it's on me! I ordered you a drink earlier so you wouldn't miss the special, but I drank it. You should have come sooner, Princess!"

Claudine's smile was soft, her eyes glassy, her movements ponderous.

"I'm good, thanks. I'm driving."

"Oh, J.P., come on, cutie! You can take a taxi!"

"You can buy me a Perrier on the rocks."

"Ah! My dear...Hugo, is it? Okay, Hugo, we'll have three Negronis on my tab, you handsome thing, you..."

"Two! None for me, thanks!"

"Ah, what a wise man. Hugo, darling, are you wise like that?"

"Yes, miss."

"Your mother must be pleased."

"Claudine, let the nice server go and don't pat him like that, he doesn't like it."

"I'm not hurting him. Look at those cheeks—shit, Adèle's calling again, that's the fourth time! Forget about a nice quiet drink, something always has to happen when I'm trying to have fun. I'll need to take this, sorry...HELLO, SWEETIE! TALK LOUDER, I'M AT A BAR...WHAT DO YOU MEAN, AGAIN? I ALMOST NEVER GO OUT!"

She put her hand over one ear and headed toward the entrance, a display of consideration that amazed me. J.P., more beautiful than ever, turned my way, untroubled by the lull in the action. I thought about his wife, the lovely Marie, and the pretty blue Italian boots she wore thanks to me.

"So how are you, Diane?"

"I'm good. Really."

"You look it."

"You do, too."

"I like your hair."

"I'm getting older, might as well own up to it."

"It brings out your eyes."

I looked down at the floor like a teenager. Oh wise Sabrina...

"Have you found another job?"

"Yes, actually, I work in a school."

"A school? Wow!"

Claudine reappeared, looking bewildered. She'd bumped into just about everyone as she made her way back to us.

"I NEED TO GO TO THE HOSPITAL!"

"What do you mean?"

"MY MOM FELL DOWN!"

"You don't need to shout, I can hear you. Where did she fall?"

"At my place, on the basement stairs."

"Is it bad?"

"Doesn't seem to be. Adèle called 911—she remembered what to do for once, amen. They're waiting together in the ER."

"Let's go."

"No, no! You stay. Relax. They think she broke her ankle or something like that. No one's dying. Fabio hasn't even shown up yet..."

"Don't be ridiculous, Claud. I'm calling a cab."

"No, stay! J.P. will look after you."

"Girls, I'll take you both over."

We turned to gaze at J.P., with his chiselled jawline and dimples perfectly centred in his cheeks.

"I insist. Let's go!"

We stopped at the bar first to settle Claudine's bill.

"Can we take the Negronis to go?"

"No, miss, but I won't charge you for them. I have a few on order, so I can give them to other customers."

"It's a funny name for a drink, come to think of it..."

"It's named after the guy who invented it."

"Oh! It's not because..."

"Not at all."

"It's kind of funny, though: if you say it fast, it sounds like—"

"Okay, Claudine, let's go!"

You guessed it: Hugo was Black. A few more words and we'd have rolled down the slippery slope of questionable humour. Better off not hanging around.

We followed J.P. to the entrance, his imposing build cutting a path through the mass of sweaty bodies that would otherwise have hindered our progress.

"Thank you for coming, see you next time!"

J.P. gave a quick nod to the hostess without slowing down at all and I raised my hand in a quick wave — "Talk to the hand!" I couldn't help thinking. Claudine walked right by her, then turned back with a sigh.

"Listen, honey, go put on some clothes. That's not a dress, it's a baby doll, and even at that —"

"Claudine, let's go!"

"Just think of the girl's mother! I bet she's not even wearing underwear!"

"Who cares? It's none of our business!"

"If she does a little nervous pee, it's gonna run straight down her leg!"

"Then let it. Come on."

J.P. pretended to rub the beard he didn't have in order to hide his laughter, but the lines around his eyes betrayed him.

In the elevator to the parking lot, Claudine reserved her seat in the car. "SHOTGUN!"

"Jesus, you'll burst my eardrums..."

After swooning over the midnight blue of J.P.'s Subaru (and making bawdy, not-so-subtle allusions to the *Emmanuelle* series), Claudine ducked in next to him.

"This must be our karma, right, Di?"

"What do you mean?"

"Having attractive men to drive us to the hospital."

She placed her hand on J.P.'s thigh as she finished the sentence.

"Claudine, *MeToo* . . ."

"You too what?"

"Hashtag MeToo, Claud, let go of his thigh, I don't think he likes it . . ."

"Oh!"

Her hand bounced up as if she'd just touched a hot stovetop. J.P. smiled. We drove for some time in the awkwardness, until the radio host's dull blather ceded the airwaves to an old Niagara tune.

"God, I haven't heard this in forever," I said.

*The girl no one ever asked to dance . . . was trying to touch the sun.* In my head, somewhere beyond the car windows, Muriel Laporte was gyrating in her circus getup, her hair on fire. We all hummed along until the girl in the song jumped off the dock at the end of winter. *Her hair, floating gently on the water . . .* Out of the corner of my eye, I could see J.P. knew all the lyrics. It made him more attractive, if that was even possible.

The sky, along with our souls, had darkened by the time we stepped out of the car, which gave us a look more suited to a hospital. We watched as the tail of the Subaru advanced into the enveloping inky blackness, a little disappointed all the same that the unfortunate circumstances had taken him from us.

After much back-and-forth between the registration desk and the security guards, we eventually found Adèle waiting in a small room in the radiology department. She jumped up when she saw her mother, the fastest I'd seen her move in the past five years.

"It's my fault, it's all my fault..."

Her chin was trembling, and she was wringing her hands in an endless uninterrupted movement.

"Okay, calm down. It was an accident."

"I should never have let her take the basket down."

"That might be, but it doesn't change anything."

"I was supposed to take it down, but I didn't feel like it. I just left it there, and—"

"Did they take X-rays?"

"Her leg was all twisted by the time I reached her, and she was moaning..."

"Still, it was an accident."

"Yeah, but if I'd just taken it down this wouldn't have happened!"

"You're right, but—"

"I'm such an idiot! I'm such an idiot! I should've just taken the damn basket down!"

"Okay, honey, calm down. What's done is done, you can't change what happened now—"

"It's always like this. I'm a wimp, I'm an idiot, I suck

at everything, I'm useless, I have no interests, everyone's always yelling at me. I just want to die—"

"Whoa! Whoa! Whoa! Okay, come here, come here..."

And then something extraordinary happened: Adèle gave in to her mother's embrace, rested her head against Claudine's shoulder, and began to cry like the child that, deep down, she still was—a vulnerable little girl stuck in the body of a woman in the making. The crack that had just opened revealed the torrent of pent-up fears and accumulated injuries that were now flooding out in a disarming jumble of feelings. Claudine sobered right up.

"Baby, do you really want to die?"

"I'm totally useless! No one needs me!"

"What about me?"

"You hate me!"

"ME? YOU THINK I HATE YOU?"

"You're always mad at me!"

"I'm not mad, I'm just trying to fire you up! I want you to move, to *live*! It kills me to see you lazing about at school, frittering away on the couch all day!"

"But I don't know how..."

"To get up?"

"To live."

"Oh, baby..."

"I hate school, I hate sports, I'm ugly—"

"No, you're not!"

"I'm not good at anything."

"That's not true."

"Then what am I good at?"

"At ... something you have yet to discover."

"Wow!"

"These things take time, it's normal."

"Well, there's nothing to discover."

"The kicks in the pants aren't going to stop, don't you worry. There are so many things you haven't tried yet."

"Like what?"

"I don't know, like ... dancing."

"*Bleah.*"

"Languages, art, travel, kung fu ..."

"*Pfff* ..."

"Whatever it is, we'll find it, okay?"

"Uh-huh."

"You scared me. You're my baby."

"Oh stop ..."

"Stop?"

"I'm fine."

"Are you sure?"

"Yes."

"Okay. I'm here for you ..."

"I know."

"Always."

"I know."

"Maybe too much?"

"Nah."

I left them to it. This part of the story belonged to them. I wouldn't have been much help, anyway. Even in his couch-potato phase (which had skipped Alexandre and Charlotte), Antoine had proven to be violently passionate. For video games, of course, but it was precisely this avenue that had given him the drive to study and work, eventually fostering in me a certain appreciation of all those exploding heads in *Mortal Kombat*.

I took the opportunity to update my children, who had all texted to ask how my first day of work had gone. Since Jacques had left, we were no longer confined—at least, not as decidedly as before—to our particular roles as parents and children. They cared for me in small ways, worried about me, wanted me to be happy. Curiously, the details I shared with each of my children were different.

To Antoine, I described the demanding schedule that would require me to rise early every day and come to terms with eating at irregular times. I had a feeling he might understand.

"Yup, you sure didn't go for a relaxing gig."

When I explained that I was at the hospital because of Claudine's mother, he wished me good luck.

To Alexandre and Justin, who'd put themselves on speakerphone so they could both listen, I talked about the children who had lost their lunch boxes, and about little manga-eyed Éléonore, who longed to play pear ball. I could tell by their tender *Oh!s* they were looking at each other and dreaming of the child they hoped to adopt one day. I couldn't help thinking, *I'm too young to be a grandmother.*

"What's all that noise in the background?"

"I'm at the hospital."

"WHAT?"

"Not for me!"

"Phew!"

"Claudine's mother fell down the stairs, and we're waiting to hear how she is."

"Is it bad?"

"Yes and no. Adèle was talking about a sprained ankle, but at her age . . ."

"Do you need anything? Have you eaten?"

"No, no. You two are so sweet. There's a cafeteria here, we'll figure it out. But thanks, boys."

I knew that all I had to do was snap my fingers and they'd turn up at the hospital with a survival kit for a three-day siege. If need be, Alexandre would send an air rescue within the hour, even if I were in Timbuktu. Having a son like him was a bit like having a father. That, or a husband from another era.

To Charlotte, I spoke about Devan and mentioned the ongoing construction—and life's coincidences.

"The same Guy?"

"Yeah, I know. They freed up some money to renovate the schools."

"Is your Guy single?"

"First, he's not 'my' Guy, and second, I'm not looking
for a relationship."

"Why not?"

"Well, because . . ."

Because to say that you're looking for a relationship
means, at least on some level — albeit indirectly — that
you want to have sex with someone you don't know.
And even though I knew she would fully approve and
even encourage me, acknowledging as much to my
daughter seemed completely inappropriate. In the
fraction of a second the ellipsis afforded me, I was
filled with hatred for the Judeo-Christian roots that
muddied my conscience and still made me associate
sex for pleasure with Evil, despite every effort to reason with myself.

" . . . I'm happy as I am."

"But that's just it — when you're happy, it means
you're ready to meet someone, Mom. You learn that
in Psych 101!"

"How would I know if he's single?"

"You ask him."

"Oh, come on . . ."

"Or you pay attention to the details."

"He doesn't wear a ring, I already checked."

"That doesn't mean a thing, Mom. People don't get married anymore. I wear one of Grandma's rings on my ring finger and I'm not married. Listen, if a guy isn't single, he'll work it into the conversation — if he's a good guy, that is. He'll mention his girlfriend this, his wife that, he'll talk about his kids, he'll say 'Bye, honey!' or just 'Me too!' before he hangs up. He'll tell you about his girlfriend's lasagna as he's taking out his lunch box . . . At some point he'll say or do something to let you know."

"And what if he doesn't?"

"Then there's a good chance he's single. Unless he's a bastard who believes he can still hit on women."

"Can't he just be a private man who doesn't like talking about his personal life?"

"That's extremely rare, and even in that case, you'd still be able to guess or suspect something by the details."

"Well, for the moment I haven't noticed much, other than a tattoo of a woman with flames on his arm."

"Tattoos are like rings, they don't mean anything either. Everyone makes mistakes. Ask him to grab a drink or a coffee, then you'll know."

"I'm a little old for all this."

"Hel-*lo*! What are you talking about? You're forty-nine. Too old for what?"

"And anyway, I didn't say I was interested in him."

"Hah! Oh yeah, right…"

"And speaking of forty-nine, I do *not* want you throwing me a fiftieth birthday party."

"I know."

"I hate that kind of thing. No gifts, no roast and toast, nothing."

My mind raced through a set of classic snapshots from parties by the decade: at twenty, my drunken stupor; at thirty, the speech/photo montage set to cheesy music (also the Botoxed smile of my stepmother pretending to think I'd been a cute ten-year-old); and then, at forty, my good (though somewhat weary) intentions, accompanied by the traditional joke basket full of adult diapers, vitamins, and pill organizers.

At fifty, I just wanted everyone to forget about me.

"Not even a little cake?"

"Not even. I've got to get back, the girls will be looking for me."

"Give me an update when you hear more about Rosanne."

"I will, I promise. I'll text you."

"Remember, you don't have to sign it."

"Char?"

"Hmm?"

"The teacher I'm assigned to is barely older than you. It seems strange."

"But that's perfect! You have experience she doesn't

and you'll be able to teach her tons of stuff about life, love, kids…"

"What worries me more is the parents giving me a hard time."

"Think about Aunt Jacinthe, it can't get worse than that."

"Hah! Oh my God, that woman…"

The doctors said it was a "pretty fracture." Aesthetics imposes its laws even on the inside. Rosanne waxed philosophical. "Pretty's always good in my book!"

They let us bring her home, provided we took good care of her and came back for X-rays in a week or two. She would stay with Claudine while she recovered, weighed down by a giant Samson boot. Adèle promised to fuss over her before we could even ask. With her school so close, it would be easy to come home for lunch and in the early afternoons. She would take care of "every tiny little thing." This left us wondering whether she'd been the one to take a fall, and headfirst. Every cloud has a silver lining.

"Who's hungry?"

"Me!"

"Me!"

"Me!"

"Should we order a pizza?"

"Half veggie!"

"And can we order a big plate of those beans?"

"Beans?"

"With the nice meat, the juice and all..."

"You mean cassoulet?"

"That's it. After everything I've been through, you know..."

Behind her mother, Claudine played air violin to indicate that Rosanne was taking advantage of our pity to place a special order. I looked at my watch.

"I'll order a pizza from Pierrot's, then swing by the bistro and grab a cassoulet to go. They must be closing soon."

"Adèle and I will take care of the old cripple."

"Hey! Watch your mouth!"

"You haven't lost your tongue, it can't be that bad."

It was a nice night, so we sat out on the balcony with our food and booze. The tinkling of glasses floated up from darkened balconies. Little dots glowed in the distance, betraying smokers taking advantage of the weather to blacken their lungs in peace. Inspired by the Shitmans, who, as usual, were peppering the silence with their sacraments, Rosanne savoured her cassoulet with quasi-religious fervour as Adèle picked through her veggie slice to ferret out any scraps of meat that, having slipped through the distracted pizzaiolo's fingers, might be lurking somewhere beneath the cheese. Cat-in-the-box, out on his night shift, was sitting like a sphinx beside Claudine's plate, knowing full well she'd toss him bits of pepperoni and crust as soon as my head was turned. Those two were always at it behind my back, often even under my nose.

Isabelle, the eldest of Simon's siblings — poor little guy, with four big sisters — came down the alley, hood pulled over her head. She slowed down when she reached our yard, glanced at the lawn, and then looked over at our small group, lit only by the few lanterns scattered across the table. We hate those big moths with fat caterpillar bodies too much to turn on more lights.

I told Isabelle that I hadn't seen their cat, Potato-B, hanging around recently. She said he was now too blind to go outside, too old for an operation, and too beat up. For animals, the end is marked by an accumulation of *toos*.

We ate and drank in near silence until the flames died down. When Laurie showed up (her mother had urged her to come by and see her grandmother), there was just one slice of veggie pizza cooling inside its soggy box. Rosanne was asleep, bundled up in the big fuzzy blanket Adèle had pulled out of their old cedar chest, and I took a picture of her to show Charlotte all was well. Cat-in-the-box had curled up into a ball on my lap.

"Hi!"

"Well look who finally showed!"

"How's Gran?"

"She's sleeping."

"Is she okay?"

"She broke her ankle, she'll be fine. How're you, sweetie?"

"Fine."

"How's the apartment?"

"It's okay."

"Just okay?"

"It's good."

"How're things with Jérémie?"

There was a long hesitation. Too long. Claudine's eyebrows did a push-up into the middle of her forehead.

"They're fine."

"You sure?"

"Yeah. Where's Adèle?"

"In her room watching Netflix."

"How is she?"

"Bah! She's doing a little soul-searching these days. You were saying…"

"Things are so-so."

"What's going on?"

"Eh, it's complicated."

"We're in no rush."

"It's no big deal."

"Things aren't going the way you'd hoped?"

"No, but they never do. You say it all the time."

Claudine made the wise decision to stay quiet. Truths told in confidence can be wild beasts.

"I *know* he works in a bar, but..."

"..."

"He didn't come home until seven Saturday morning."

"SEVEN?!"

"*Shhhh!*"

"What time do bars close?"

"Three, same as always. But it's his job to close out the cash, do inventory, clean up the place..."

"Those counters must be *real* shiny!"

"He said he fell asleep in a booth after he ate."

"At the bar?"

"There are couches in the cigar room, that's where they balance the cash."

"He fell asleep counting his money?"

"That's what he said."

"He must've felt bad when he came home?"

"Not any worse than the other times."

"It wasn't the first time?"

"The third."

"And you believe him?"

"Of course I don't, it's total bullshit. Especially

since I turned on his mobile tracking and I know he wasn't there."

"I don't understand."

"I can see his cell on mine, so I know where he is in real time, and he wasn't there. He left the bar at four."

"You can see him walking on your phone?"

"I can see where he is, yeah."

"And where was he?"

"Guess."

"Strippers?"

"Come *on*, Mom!"

Laurie explained that she'd discovered her boyfriend was blowing part of his two or three hundred bucks in tip money at after-hours clubs, semi-secret places where people can keep partying after the bars close. The only "afters" I'd been to were for onion rings at the local snack bar, washed down with a shot of dishwater coffee.

"Do you seriously think he's going there just to drink?"

"If I asked, that's what he'd say."

"Well, ask!"

"I can't!"

"Why not?"

"Because I'm not supposed to know he wasn't at the bar."

"But you do!"

"But if I tell him I know he wasn't at the bar, he'll

suspect I'm tracking him and he'll look through his phone and flip out and block me. So I have to stop tracking him, see?"

" . . . "

"I pretend to believe him so he doesn't realize I'm tracking him."

"That's so twisted!"

"Yeah, but for now I don't have a choice."

"Call him on it!"

"I don't want to."

"Why not?"

"Because. It might not be what we think."

"Maybe not, you're right. You're the boss, I guess."

"And this boss'll have a glass of what you're having."

I indicated to Claudine not to move, that I'd take care of it. We couldn't risk stirring the air around us too much, or Laurie might curl up and be consumed by her anguish.

By the time I returned with the glass of rosé, Laurie was crying, head buried in her mother's embrace. Claudine, loving her first-born with all her strength, silently enveloped her in a big, generous embrace, eyes brimming with tears. I went back to the kitchen to make myself scarce.

# 7

## In which Miss Sophie
## spends a long time in the bathroom

The following week, I opted to attend my very first professional development day, presented by the school board and entitled, "Listen, Defuse, Guide." The PD day (which, to my great surprise, had been stuck smack in the middle of the week) wouldn't require the services of all the aides because many of the older students had chosen to stay home and, with their great sense of independence — and mastery of the iPad — look after themselves. I'd chosen to see how a series of *Eat, Pray, Love*–style workshops could equip me to face the Devans of the world. Miss Sophie had also registered, which I thought would provide an opportunity for us to get to know one another better.

When I saw her standing in front of the entrance to

the Convention Centre, pretty and fresh-faced, I hardly recognized her. She was perched on four-inch heels and wearing an exquisite jumpsuit that offered a complete, sculpted outline of the human form. On their way inside, everyone who passed by looked her over from head to toe, front to back. The body she hid daily underneath ordinary, functional clothing was visible in all its splendour. I didn't even have the strength to be jealous.

"Ah, Diane! I'm so glad you're here!"

"My, don't you look great!"

"I have a big favour to ask."

She was as jumpy as a little girl, nervously biting her lip.

"Could you pick up my folder for me?"

"What folder?"

"We always get a folder with our name on it at the beginning of the day. That's where they put the papers for the workshops. It's a way to take attendance."

"Okay."

"If we don't show up, they'll dock our paycheque..."

"Oh!"

"So it would be a really, really big help if they thought I was here today. It's not just about the money..."

Her pleading eyes met mine, and I restrained a violent urge to ask what else it was about. I wanted to be young and cool like her, to pretend I understood what was going on.

"I get it. But can't you pick up your folder and then sneak out?"

"There's a form to fill out after each workshop."

"Oh! So you're asking me to . . ."

"Yeah, but it's only a sentence or two, like 'Awesome idea, can't wait to try this in class! Thank you!' I always write stuff like that. They won't notice the handwriting's not the same."

It took some nerve to ask me to lie and spend the day cheating the system on her behalf. But I was cool.

"No worries, I'll take care of it."

"You could tell them I went to the bathroom and asked you to pick up my folder . . ."

"Will they believe me?"

"Well . . . it might help if you show this."

She held out a small handbag that was a questionable shade of purple.

"A purse?"

"Yes, to hold while I'm in the bathroom. There's a wallet inside with cards and an old driver's licence, just in case."

"But women usually take their purse into the bathroom, don't they?"

"Not for a quick pee."

"And does this usually work?"

"I don't know, I'm hoping it will. I have a really important meeting today . . ."

"Okay, give it to me."

"Are you sure?"

"Sure. The meeting sounds really important, go ahead."

"Thanks, you're the best."

"Don't worry about it. Now get out of here."

"I owe you."

She turned to go.

"Sophie?"

"Uh-huh?"

"Can I ask you something?"

Her smile fell.

"Uh...sure."

"Do you actually use this purse? It's hideous."

"Hah! No, but it was a gift, so I can't get rid of it."

"What if I'd said no?"

"I knew you'd say yes."

She threw me a cute smile before dashing out into the street, off to do whatever was so important she'd risked putting her fate into the hands of a near-stranger. I rummaged through the purse and found the wallet and licence: 1993. I'd been pregnant with my second.

Before stepping through the doors of the air-conditioned auditorium where some hyperactive speaker running on turmeric fumes was preparing to give us a little pep talk, we were all handed, as expected, a folder containing the workshop materials and...a mood ring to track our spirits throughout the day — in case we felt unhappier than we really were. Two of the women ahead of me put theirs on, whispering.

"Look, it's black. I'm angry."

"Mine's pink. It says 'cool.'"

"Someone in charge must have a dentist for a brother-in-law, with boxes of these rings to offload..."

My heart was racing by the time my turn came.

"Diane Delaunais, A-I-S," I said. "And I'll grab Sophie Maheu's folder, too. We're together. We work with the same classroom."

"Participants have to pick up their own folders."

I held up the little purple purse and gave what I hoped was a conspiratorial wink.

"It couldn't wait. I can show you her ID if you'd like..."

She returned my wink and handed over my imaginary friend's folder without asking for proof. Easy-peasy. I have a face that inspires confidence; that's how it is when you're boring. I stuffed Sophie's things into my own purse, the giant kind moms use because, even twenty years after the last diaper, they never learned how to get by with a smaller one.

On the stage, lit as if the Disney princesses themselves would be making an appearance, bunches of helium-filled balloons framed the podium where a microphone stood waiting. Perfect for a car salesman, a master of ceremonies, or a birthday clown. When the person in charge greeted us with a vigorous "Hello everybody! Ready to get down to business?" I knew it would be a long, long day. I looked down at my ring. Amber = worried: more clairvoyant than I had given it credit for.

The first workshop lasted an hour and a half. We took ten minutes to introduce ourselves, twenty minutes to rate our level of motivation on a scale of one to ten (I said eight to be nice and keep the conversation short, but I'd been at two and a half since the opening remarks in the auditorium), fifteen minutes on a case study (the child who "doesn't hear" the rules), a fifteen-minute break, a further fifteen minutes on a second case study (the child who wants to negotiate the rules), and the rest to re-evaluate our level of motivation and then share our answers with the group. I was the only one not to change my rating, lauding the workshop leader with over-the-top compliments and thanking her for the outstanding information (some rules can be established, others not, and even at that it depends on the child) and her incredible organizational skills. At least in this last regard, she'd been flawless: every segment of her workshop, though three-quarters of them were useless, had been rigorously timed. When it came to our questionnaires, I jotted down vague stock comments that were diametrically opposed: "Thank you! I learned a lot of interesting things." And "Too much *blah blah* and not enough content, though well organized." That was from Miss Sophie, of course.

By the fourth and final workshop of the day, my tally of useful minutes hadn't even done a full turn of the clock. My ring had taken me through a range of emotions, though predominantly purple = impatient, before landing on green = anxious. I hadn't an ounce of hope left as I walked into room 212, other than that we might be spared from silly, slightly infantilizing games. The moderator started right on time, while some of the participants were still standing.

"My name is Rachelle. I've been a family psychologist for twenty-seven years, and I also do work within the school system. Thank you all for coming. Every day, each of you is dealing with behaviours that range from unpleasant, punishable, shameful, to downright mean, hateful, even devilish..."

A tinkle of laughter rang out across the room. No kid gloves and lace this time — we would gladly crush all the eggshells we were walking on.

"We could spend the rest of the day detailing these behaviours. I'm sure it would help to vent—"

Magnificent teeth, a round face, a voice full of composure — she was solid. About fifty, the perfect age.

"—but that wouldn't work in the long term. The bottom line is that a child always gains something from negative behaviour. Always. What that is might not be so obvious, but make no mistake — children gain something, otherwise they wouldn't act out. And usually the gain corresponds to a need."

Eight hands shot up into the air.

"Yes?"

"I don't see what a child gains when there's a punishment involved."

"And your name is...?"

"Jocelyne."

"Give me an example of a punishment, Jocelyne."

"Well...take a kid who pushes in line when it's time for recess. I have one like that. He's always pushing, at every recess, it's the same thing every day. Kid's a real pain in the ass..."

"What do you do when that happens?"

"I give him a time out and he loses his recess."

"Where is the time out?"

"We make him sit right by the door. He's easier to watch that way."

"You leave him there all by himself?"

"No, at least not for the whole recess. He needs to learn why he's there, so we go over the rules, either me or one of my colleagues. I explain all over again, give him an earful..."

Rachelle's face stretched into a smile with no teeth, as if to say, *Aha!*

"But really, who'd want a time out and a lecture? It's boring as hell!"

"Clearly not for him. He gets lots of attention that way. Getting yelled at is better than being ignored. That child gains an adult all to himself, an opportunity he might not have at home. And a kind adult, at that. Does he have any friends?"

"Hard to say."

"Probably not a ton."

The air was filled with murmurs of "Oh!" and "Ah!" that swung between astonishment and disbelief. It was both so simple and so hard to understand.

"What might seem to us like a punishment can feel like preferential treatment to a child craving attention. But the truth might be even simpler than that: lots of children hate recess. They're the last ones chosen for soccer teams — actually, *chosen* is a big word. Often they're forced to play for the smaller team, they're pushed off the play structures, they're bullied. They wind up throwing pebbles along the fence, waiting for recess to end, wishing it would go by fast. Some don't have any friends, others don't have a snack or the right clothes for outside — you know better than me . . . Finding a way to skip recess and spend it elsewhere can be a blessing for them."

"Then what do I do with him?" Jocelyne asked.

"Try to figure out what he's looking for in the

punishment. Time out in the corner isn't working; you need to find something else."

"How?"

"There's no magic recipe, it depends on the child's needs. I have ideas for avenues to explore, lots of great stories, too, but no miracles. Kateri Tekakwitha doesn't work for social services..."

She presented us with a list of problematic behaviours and asked us to first try to understand what the child gained by acting out. We couldn't intervene until we attacked the knot, the root of the issue. Rachelle dissected each of our ideas—she was the epitome of the expression "I wasn't born yesterday"—prompting us to travel long-forgotten paths and providing numerous examples of small changes that led to big results as she did so. No two stories were alike, and the solutions were often found off-trail on side roads cleared through trial and error. One of these cases featured a teacher's aide who'd managed to mollify one of the worst troublemakers in her class, a kid for whom punishments had long ceased to be effective, through a one-on-one game of Mille Bornes after school. They'd moved on to UNO, backgammon, Chinese checkers, Yum, and, in grade 6, even cribbage. The games had served as a lightning rod—the pawns, cards, and fingers diverted the current, giving some respite to the authorities charged with his academic fulfillment. This particular solution, however, did little for other children who ostensibly had the same type of problems. The knot could be anywhere, in a kid's misguided brain or a lunch box, and the solutions varied just as much. I could have listened to Rachelle for hours, and when the workshop ended, I glanced down at my ring to see if it glowed "disappointed." Miss Sophie was full of praise. From the distant bathroom stall where she'd spent the day, she had "totally freaked out, everything was so interesting!"

You're only young once.

All this talk of unpleasant behaviours had me thinking, and memories flooded back to me like the slimy seaweed-capped waves on which my son Antoine had surfed. I pictured his messy room, his long apathetic days, and my fruitless attempts at speeches meant to spur him into action. I thought back to all the times he had been late, had earned detentions, had failed exams, and to the harsh words—"hopeless case," "lazy bum"—that manifested a reality we were powerless to change. I had never imagined his behaviour would earn him anything other than the reprimands he scoffed at in such despair. What is to be gained by challenging our loved ones' nearly total inertia? What is the endgame of doing nothing? Adèle offered us a chance to ask ourselves these questions every day, though we never bothered to find the answers. I'd never realized that behind her lethargy, something was missing. Now it dawned on me that I might have spent twenty years prodding and lecturing a son who chose to communicate his distress through indolence. I ran to take refuge in my car. My phone, almost dead, was waiting for me in the cup holder. Claudine had tried to reach me but hadn't left a message. Whatever it was couldn't be that important. I called Antoine.

"Hi, baby, it's your mom!"

"Uh...hello."

"Is something wrong?"

"No, no. It's just...baby?"

"Oh, it just came out."

"I'm still at work, Mom. Can I call you back?"

"Do you have two minutes? It's just a quick question."

"Okay, two minutes. I'm with a colleague."

"I'll be fast. I was wondering... when you were young, when you were little—actually, even while you were growing up..."

"Oh boy!"

"...did you ever feel you were missing something, Antoine? I'm not talking about clothes or food. Something more...inside, maybe?"

"Uhh..."

"Hang on, let me put it another way. I was wondering if your behaviour earned you access to something you needed but couldn't express—sometimes people don't even realize what they're doing. Maybe something was going on that your father and I couldn't see, some-thing we didn't understand, and you might have been acting out in order to fulfill that need. I don't know if you see what I mean..."

"Mom, I'll call you back."

"Okay, baby."

My ring was turquoise.

"CALM? I'M *CALM*?!"

Without looking, I hurled the ring with all my might through the car window. Resilient in its cheap plastic, arrogant like the bullshit it was, it ricocheted off the car parked next to mine and flew back through the window to land at my feet and roll beneath my seat. I reached as far back as I could, but it was useless: the ring had slipped into a crack in the floor mat, eluding my destructive urge. To calm down, I pictured myself pounding it to dust with the sledgehammer. I'd come to learn how to be a better aide, and I left convinced I'd been a bad mother.


"Hello, Malika!"

"Diane? My God, what's the occasion?"

I'd never been the sort of pushy mother-in-law who turns up unexpectedly. Malika's astonishment assured me of this. But despite the arsenal of good intentions I'd brought to my son's apartment, my eyes couldn't help surveying the state of the balcony: the overflowing garbage can, the pile of soggy cardboard boxes, the withered plants, the tightly spun cobwebs dotted with decomposing flies, the layers of dead leaves already beginning to rot, the rusty nails, the Kit Kat wrapper stuck fast to the ground by some unidentified substance . . . How had this happened? And why? I couldn't understand it. In the past three decades, the most I'd ever slacked off with the chores had been to let the grass grow until it became hay the year Jacques and I separated.

"I came by to see Antoine, but I know he's not back yet. I was wondering if I could wait for him here."

"Of course you can! Come on in. Nothing serious, I hope?"

"No, just dropping by."

My visit had been subconsciously orchestrated. I needed to see Antoine in his element, to stick my nose into his daily life without him scrambling to please me — and, I was smart enough to recognize, possibly only me.

"It smells good in here! What are you making?"

"Vegetarian chili."

"Vegetarian?"

"I'm not telling Antoine; he won't even realize it's vegetarian. I crumbled up some tofu, and with all the spices and the sauce it's just like meat. I did the same thing with the spaghetti the other day, and he had no idea."

"You'll have to show me how. Everyone's going vegetarian these days."

Malika was a graphic designer and she often worked from home. At the moment, her office was set up on the kitchen table between dirty dishes, a full laundry basket, and pop cans of Matcha tea over which fruit flies circled erratically. With multimedia companies fighting over Antoine, he and Malika could have afforded a larger apartment or even bought their own place, but they were happy in their little cocoon. My daughter-in-law looked beautiful, relaxed—as beautiful as the term "daughter-in-law" is ugly. She moved around the kitchen in a single fluid motion, at one with the mess that was as comfortable for her and my son as it was overwhelming to me.

"I don't want to interrupt your work. Do what you have to and don't worry about me. Maybe I could fold your laundry while I wait?"

"Why don't you relax? You just got off work."

"Bah! It was a professional development day. Plus, folding helps me unwind."

"How is school? Do you like it?"

"Yes! Oh yes, I love it. It's . . . challenging."

"I bet it helps that you had your own kids?"

"On some level, yes, but the world is completely different today."

"What's changed?"

"Well..."

I held back from sharing what was on my mind as I folded bath towels that must have been white before they were repeatedly washed with the darks.

"...I'm not sure, exactly. I didn't work in a school back then, so I can't really compare."

"I hear kids can't concentrate because of all the screen time."

"I'm in the kindergarten, and kids that age never have a long attention span. It's normal. But they're adorable. Some have more energy than others, of course...But one thing's for sure—I'm never going back to an office."

When Antoine walked in and saw his underwear piled neatly on the table, I kicked myself for not knowing how to sit on my hands and wait.

"Man, I tried calling you back like ten times!"

"My phone! I must have left it in the car. I'm always forgetting it."

"You almost had me worried."

"I'm sorry, baby, you know how I am with my phone..."

"So what is this, some existential crisis?"

"Oh stop, it was just a question. I wanted to know, so I could understand better."

"I have to grab some things from the corner store," said Malika. "The chili's simmering, just keep an eye on it, okay?"

And then Antoine and I were alone, left to stare at one another. The question I'd wanted to ask an hour earlier, one that seemed so simple at the time, had disintegrated into a jumble of unintelligible syllables. Fortunately, he didn't wait for me to finish.

"Mom, I'm just not like Alex and Char. I'm not *perfect*."

"Nobody ever asked you to be perfect!"

"Maybe not, but I was stuck between two kids who were perfect, so everything I wasn't stood out all the more. It's stressful, being surrounded by perfect people when you're just...normal."

"Oh, baby..."

"And when I tried, it never worked anyway."

"Antoine, that's terrible..."

"But I didn't think about it, Mom. I was just me, and I was fine with that. I'm only telling you this because you asked me earlier, and I started thinking about it in the car so I could answer, but that's not actually how I saw things at the time. It didn't occur to me, or at least not like that. Maybe I did look lazy by comparison—they were high achievers in kindergarten—but what could I do?"

I sat down on a chair that already held a coat, a scarf, and a reusable flower-patterned grocery bag.

"Plus, there was Alex to protect, Char to coddle... Don't cry, Mom, there wasn't anything missing, I was happy. I *am* happy..."

"It hurts me to picture you growing up believing you weren't 'perfect,' that you weren't as good as the other two . . ."

"But I *didn't*, that's what I'm telling you. And it won't change anything, anyway."

"Yes, but—"

"Aw, come here."

When Malika arrived, my imperfect baby was consoling me in his big arms. She smacked her forehead.

"I forgot to pick up a few Coronas to go with the chili!" she said and headed out again.

I declined their offer to stay for dinner. I hadn't called ahead, and it was impolite to barge in like that. At any rate, I couldn't see how all three of us would have fit. Once the door closed behind me, I bent to pick up the Kit Kat wrapper and stuffed it in my pocket.

For the first time since we'd separated, I needed to speak to Jacques. I couldn't call Claudine, because she'd fall over herself telling me I was the best mother in the world. In the moment, I wanted to hear words with the ring of truth from someone inside the nest. And there was no denying it: I also needed to unburden myself and distribute some of the weight to the other guilty party. I pulled out my phone once I'd returned to my car.

"We punished him too much. We should have realized it wasn't helping."

"Diane, we punished him when he deserved to be

punished. We didn't treat him any differently than the others. The rules were the same for everybody."

"Are you sure?"

"He just had a harder time following them."

"It's not that he broke the rules, he just . . . didn't do *anything*."

"It amounted to the same thing. If we asked him to do something and he didn't do it, he had to deal with the consequences."

"But he was trying to provoke us, it was like self-sabotage! He felt he wasn't as good as the other two, and pushing our buttons was a way to tell us he wasn't like them!"

"We never told him he wasn't as good as the others! He just wasn't good at the same things. Look, today he's a whiz with computers. He doesn't like sports, he never will—"

"That's my fault."

"—but he's more creative than the others. Okay, he cuts corners when it comes to organization, the house—"

"His appearance, too, a bit."

"—but he's extremely rigorous in his work, he's responsible . . ."

I was annoyed with myself. Why couldn't I have found simple, comforting words like these instead of tearfully babbling away like a repentant mother late to the game? We'd treated Antoine fairly, we'd loved him just as much as the others. He was different, but he had been no less successful. He possessed the uncomplicated joy of someone who lets himself be pushed around, yet knows when to brake and change course.

"Hang on a sec, Charlene's waving at me. Looks important."

I had been so consumed by our conversation as introspective parents sifting through the past that I'd almost forgotten Jacques was now my ex, that his wife had just banished her Prince on the Hill. The moment I pictured Bimbo, I hung up without an ounce of hesitation or remorse. I'd already earned a reputation for being a psycho, and didn't care what Jacques thought. He'd calmed me down, that was true, but at so little cost I didn't feel any compulsion to be grateful. In the great book of our shared history, his surfeit of dull common sense could fill an abyss. So I made like a kid and sent a brief text to Claudine:

temporary solution asap

No capital letters, no verb, no punctuation, unsigned.

After the second bottle of pink temporary solution — Rosanne would no longer drink anything else — Adèle marched onto the balcony, eyes blazing. The three of us had more or less concluded we'd done the best we could with our children. The wine had numbed our remaining guilt.

"My hair straightener died!"

"My condolences," Claudine said.

"How can I go out looking like this?"

"You say that like it's my fault."

"You wouldn't buy me a new one the other day."

"Because the one you have still worked!"

"Well, it was cheap, and now it doesn't!"

"Where are you going, anyway?"

"To Noémie's."

"Her annoying little sister won't be there?"

"Who cares?"

"Why can't you go to Noémie's with your natural hair?"

"Because I look like a lunatic!"

"It's only Noémie..."

"Yeah, but I'll have to take the bus since you're still drinking and won't be able to give me a ride because you're too hammered."

Claudine threw her a classic need-to-shit smile that gave her the strength to pretend she hadn't heard anything.

"You don't look like a lunatic. Your hair is wavy like mine, sweetie."

"That's why I need to straighten it. Otherwise I look like the monkey in *The Croods*."

Big gulp of wine, deep breath.

"Your grandmother and I have the same hair, and we've never straightened it. There was no such thing back in our day..."

"Yeah, we know, and you only had oranges at Christmas, too."

"We still managed to marry."

"Just not to stay married, in your case."

Rosanne sat bolt upright. "Don't you be fresh to your mama!"

"It was only a joke."

"A bad one. Apologize."

"But..."

"NOW!"

"Sorry..."

Adèle wilted before her grandmother. She closed her mouth, dropped her arms, and lowered her eyes. The dead straightener swung from the end of its cord like a hanged man.

"Only a bloody fool thinks hair could end a marriage... We didn't have all these contraptions back in my day, but we still got by. We fixed and we mended damn near everything. For the rest, we made do. Before we ever had a dryer, your granddad used to wedge diapers in the car windows and drive around like that until they were dry, to give you some idea."

"What, you didn't have pharmacies?"

"They were cloth diapers, you had to empty and wash them."

"Gross!"

"Same thing for lady napkins."

"No details, please!"

"Run and get the iron and ironing board, I'll show you how to do your hair."

"Not with a clothes iron!"

"Why not?"

"It's for *clothes.*"

"Clothes, hair, you get the wrinkles out the same way."

"Don't get up, Ma. Your foot."

"The day I can't get up anymore is the day you bury me."

"I thought you wanted to be cremated."

"It's just an expression."

Once Rosanne and Adèle were inside, Claudine looked over at me sharply.

"Do you think I look like a monkey?"

"Hmm . . . Not when you talk."

"Maybe that's the problem."

"What problem?"

"With my date."

"What date?"

"Marc, the guy from Tinder."

"When's the date?"

"It was at noon."

"Today?"

"Uh-huh."

"You didn't tell me!"

"We decided to get lunch. Spur of the moment. He wanted to meet up before going out for dinner and diving into all that."

"And you didn't call me?"

"Three times."

"Shit! I didn't see it."

"No worries, I had nothing to say."

"You didn't go?"

"I did."

"He didn't show up?"

"Of course he did, or I wouldn't be asking about my hair."

"True. Okay, well?"

"He left."

"What do you mean, he left?"

"I saw him come into the restaurant…"

"Which one?"

"Chez Édouard. I got a table by the window, way in the back. He didn't look much like his picture."

"No? Was he fatter?"

"Older, maybe, but I still recognized him."

"Attractive?"

"Hard to say. Well dressed..."

"Okay."

"I told him what I'd be wearing and roughly where I'd be sitting, so he saw me. He thanked the hostess who greeted him, he took a step in my direction...he looked right at me, I smiled..." She stared ahead as she replayed the nightmare, her free hand cupped around her neck. "...and he just left."

"What? He didn't walk over to your table?"

"No."

"He didn't say anything to you?"

"No. He turned around and walked out the way he came in."

"What a scumbag!"

"Message received, I'll give him that."

"But that's so rude! He could've taken a few minutes to sit down with you..."

"And say what? 'Sorry, but this won't work. I don't like fatties.'"

"You're not fat."

"Diane..."

"People come in more than two sizes."

"When a guy does a one-eighty just at the sight of you, it's not because he thinks you're a dummy."

"He's an asshole. Period."

"Or he didn't like my monkey hair."

She gulped down the two inches of wine oxidizing at the bottom of her glass.

"Just forget all those shitty apps, Claud."

"And do what, sign up for a jogging club?"

"Why not? You can learn, just like you would anything else."

"Look who's talking."

"As it happens, I have some trainers at home collecting dust."

"Hey, speaking of being lame … Do you think I have a drinking problem?"

"We do drink a lot."

" 'We'? You're funny. I."

"Either way."

"Do you think I'm an alcoholic?"

"From a clinical perspective, yes. Me too. In real life…"

"Okay, we'll go with the goddamn rule of three: Monday, Tuesday, and Wednesday we don't drink. That leaves us happy hour on Thursday and long weekends."

"We could even replace a cocktail with a jog around the block."

"Whoa there! One battle at a time."


When I returned the lovely Sophie's horrible purse the next day, she looked at me with the sad eyes of a caged bear. The excitement that had fluttered the flounces of her jumpsuit a day earlier had been extinguished, giving her cheeks a chalky look. During our five-minute breaks between shifts, I wasn't able to make her laugh once as I told her all the silly things she'd written on the workshop questionnaires. Nor did I find the words to chip away at our overly polite relationship.

# 8

## In which I worship
## a soggy twenty-dollar bill

Mini Éléonore's father had taken things into his own hands: he'd found a decent cobbler who'd agreed to make a leather strap long enough so that kids who were Éléonore's size could reach the pear ball with their fists. He'd even found time to visit the schoolyard the previous evening and test the strap to make sure it worked. It was such a simple solution that everyone was kicking themselves for not having thought of it earlier. The kind, resourceful father—an engineer, no surprise there—was all smiles when he left that morning, under the admiring eyelash-batting of his daughter (and all the middle-aged ladies in the yard, myself included). An adorable dad who outshined all the rest. In another era, a long, long time ago, I'd married a guy like that—and had him stolen out from under me. I felt for the engineer's wife.

Everything was proceeding swimmingly that morning until Kathleen, the much less adorable teacher of grade 6B, stuck her nose in.

"There aren't enough little kids for us to reserve one of the three poles just for them."

"Oh, come on, we're not about to start counting..."

"That's exactly it. If we want to be fair, then we have to count heads. There are four hundred and fifty students in the school and only around twenty-five of them are too small for the regular balls. That's not even five percent! We can't give them thirty-three percent of the poles."

"But they want to play pear ball, too!"

"They'll play when they're tall enough. All the others had to wait."

"Wow! Nothing like changing with the times..."

"They can't even hit the ball."

"We don't know that, they never had a chance to try!"

"They can use the play structures. They're old enough to climb, just not to hit."

"But the play structures are full of bigger kids who push the little ones off!"

"Then they can play with broken pieces of asphalt."

A real grinch. A bilious husk wholly devoted to hate and bickering. If mean people are fundamentally unhappy, then it was evident she'd been through hell and back at some point in her life. Had the issue been between just the two of us, I'd have dropped the whole thing.

"Plus, it's not the school's equipment. If there's an accident, we'll be in trouble."

"Oh my gosh, we're talking about one strap that's slightly longer than the others."

"Well, maybe they don't make them longer because it's dangerous!"

"Whoooo! Watch out for *Massacre of the Strap!*"

Linda joined me, an ally I'd very soon be needing.

*"Amityville, the Strap of the Devil!"*

But the big sourpuss didn't fluster easily. She shot back with a simple yet categorical argument as she ripped the strap from Linda's hands.

"At any rate, it's the administration's decision to make."

The boring woman I'd been before probably wouldn't have done anything. But the new one resolutely held out her hand and gritted her teeth, her that's-it jiggling.

"Hand over the strap."

"It's up to the administration..."

"HAND IT OVER!"

There was no way she was walking away with it; the risk of an X-ACTO knife "accidentally" plunging into the precious item was too great. She held it out slowly—too slowly. I yanked it from her grip as soon as

I felt the leather against my fingers, and then promptly returned to my kindergarteners, where the saddest five percent of kids I'd ever seen were waiting for me. In the midst of the dismayed, silent group—the only sound was Devan striking rocks together, trying to set the school on fire—Éléonore twisted the hem of her dress in her tiny fingers, lips quivering. Her father's strap had nearly slipped away. Not on my watch. I marched over to the third pole, which was being one hundred percent monopolized by the big kids, and, as if the order came all the way from up on high, bellowed, "Okay, time to change the ball!"

"Hey! We were waiting our turn!"

"You won't lose your turn, you'll just have to play on your knees. And if you don't like it, there are two other lines. Or you can climb on the play structures. Or play with broken pieces of asphalt."

Once the ball had been attached, I turned to Miss Kathleen and her funereal pout over on the concrete landing, where she was observing the scene. I threw her a real estate agent's smile. I knew, of course, that my defiance was tantamount to a declaration of war, but lately life had given me a break from hostilities and I was thrilled by this initial victory. And to my kindergarteners, I was the hero of the day.

• • •

I was still basking in my glory when, as I was leaving the building after lunch, I crossed paths with a very tiny, very wrinkled old woman clutching the gum-covered bannister with both hands as she painfully made her way up the stairs. Her skin and hair were blue-grey, her clothing mint green, and she was wearing a shawl that very much resembled a couch throw. There weren't too many possibilities: she was a great-grandmother coming to pick up her great-grandson for a dentist appointment, a speaker coming to talk about the realities of old people abandoned to long-term care homes, or a woman with Alzheimer's who was a little lost. I approached her gently.

"Hello, ma'am!"

"Oh! Hello...hello..."

"Can I help you up the stairs?"

"I didn't expect there to be so many. That would be lovely, thank you."

"Here, hold my arm."

"How nice, such a strong arm...You're in the prime of life, it's a beautiful thing."

She patted my forearm gently to test out its youthful vigour. It was the first time anyone had talked about my bulges in terms of strength. If I could have given her a few of my pounds, we would have both benefited.

"Are you here to pick up a student?"

"No, no, unfortunately not. I need to see someone."

"Shall I take you to the secretary's office?"

"I'm not sure where to go, but we can start there."

"Who do you need to see?"

"A strong man would be nice."

"A strong man?"

Her eyes completely disappeared beneath all the wrinkles. It was her way of laughing.

"I noticed they're doing renovations to the school. All day long I see big trucks going by and men in those hard hats. I live right next door."

"The house with the shutters?"

"That's the one."

"It's very charming."

"If one of the workers could come by my place, I have a little favour to ask—I'd pay, of course, I'm not here to beg."

"What sort of favour?"

"I need someone to pull up the living room carpet."

"Ah, those collect dust."

"Oh yes! Dust and everything else."

"Do you have allergies?"

"No, no, no, those didn't exist back in my day, though we did have all the rest. Ugly critters with pretty names...kept us on our toes. It's an old, old carpet."

"How long have you had it?"

"Forever."

This placed it somewhere between the two world

wars, considering that the words *old, old* coming from a woman of such a venerable age clearly launched us back a few generations, well before the invention of the hair straightener and disposable diapers, to the days when people ate paupers' meals every night of the week.

"Listen, I'll find you a chair and go talk to the guys. I know them, they're as gentle as lambs, and one of them might be interested in your offer. It'll save you a trip through the school yard and another flight of stairs."

"That's so kind of you, dear. How can I refuse? I'm not opposed to dying, but only once I've pulled up the carpet."

"Your name?"

"Madeleine. Madeleine Tremblay."

I settled her into a little chair with tennis ball slippers and went to find the most attractive tattooed man in the yard. He was doing some sort of thing with some sort of tool—that's as much detail as I can offer with any authority.

"Hey, Guy, can I talk to you for a sec?"

"Hey, Lady Di!"

"There's a woman in the secretary's office, Ms. Tremblay, she lives in the little house next door..."

"Is it the noise?"

"No, it's about a carpet. She's looking for a strong man to pull up her living room carpet."

"Is it tacked or glued?"

"Uh... I didn't ask."

"Okay."

"Could one of your guys do it after his shift? It's just next door, and she's offering to pay."

"JOHNNY? I'M TAKING TWO MINUTES! WAIT FOR ME BEFORE YOU LOWER THE DUMP! Okay, I'll go have a look."

The old woman hadn't moved a muscle, as if I'd put her in time out. She seemed delighted with the size of the man I'd dug up for her, and her little mouth formed a big, astonished "Oh!"

"*Mon Dieu!*"

"Hello, ma'am!"

She placed both her hands into the one he extended, like an animal huddling for warmth. Guy could easily have carried the small sack of bones across the short distance to her house like a young bride. But instead, we walked patiently down the stairs, taking them one by one, both feet flat on each step as we gradually made our way over to her door.

"Keep your shoes on or you'll get your socks dirty."

The smell overwhelmed us immediately. It felt like I'd inhaled a giant gulp of acid. A trio of tabby cats met us at the door like gatekeepers. Guy gave me a sidelong glance and whispered "ammonia." A charming first date. He took off his quilted flannel jacket and hung it on a hook in the hall.

"How many cats do you have, Ms. Tremblay?"

"Oh, four or five."

Without moving or peering through the darkness, I could already count six. It appeared there were many more than she thought.

"One of the window panes in the kitchen is open, so the cats come and go as they please. It's hard to keep track of them."

"Wouldn't it be better to close it?"

"It's stuck."

"How long has it been stuck?"

"Forever."

"I'm sure we can fix that."

I thought of those horror stories in which old people, long dead and forgotten, end up being eaten by their cat, dog, or hamster. A shiver went through me, even though, in reality, there was almost nothing to eat on this woman. Guy ran a hand over his face, presumably wondering where to start. Our feet sank with a disturbing *squelch* into parts of the carpet that had undoubtedly once been nice and soft. I looked up automatically, searching for a water leak. The ceiling was laced with cracks, the paint peeling in large petals here and there that hung by a thread. But no sign of a leak.

"We'll have to move the furniture . . . I'll need my tools, it's tacked down . . . Okay, I'll be right back."

"Right now? You can send someone over later, can't you?"

He cocked his head a few degrees and gave a half-hearted smile. Clearly, this couldn't wait.

"I'll give the guys a few instructions and come right back."

"Okay. Tell me what to do—I could move the furniture in the meantime?"

"Start in the back, with the chairs. Wait for me to help with the buffet—and don't overdo it, I'll take care of the rest."

*Don't overdo it.* I felt precious. Madeleine was thrilled. She couldn't stop thanking us and apologizing for not having any food to offer us. In another era, there would have been *sucre à la crème*, date squares, meatloaf—and her specialty, cinnamon buns.

"Do you have children?"

"Everyone's been dead for years. My sons, too. Adrien at fifty-six, Paul at seventy-two. That's them in the photographs."

"I'm sorry."

"They say you just have to accept it when God calls His people back. Which I could understand for my husband, my brothers and sisters, and all the others . . . but not for my sons. Never for them. He came for us in the wrong order. He had no right to, and I never forgave Him for it . . . That's why He's forcing me to keep on living. It's my punishment. He teaches us, but He doesn't like being taught."

A big black cat with singed fur was rubbing up against my leg, ass in the air. I ventured a quick pat, but when I thought of all the parasites that could be hiding in his shaggy coat, my hand snapped back as if I'd stuck it into an electrical outlet.

"Do you feed all these cats?"

"No, they fend for themselves. There's all kinds of vermin outside. Sometimes they bring me gifts."

She giggled, her hand over her mouth. I thought: avian flu, *E. coli*, salmonella, the whole gamut of sneaky diseases that can worm their way into our water, our bodies, our brains.

"But I give them dry food in winter, when they can't even find so much as a fly to eat."

"Do you do your own shopping?"

"No, Malik at the pharmacy delivers my order. He's a nice boy. He brings groceries over with my medication. You can find everything at a pharmacy today, or everything I eat, at any rate."

"You order food from the pharmacy?"

"Oh, I'm not difficult."

"But they don't sell fruits or vegetables..."

"I get them canned. They have mixed vegetables, pears in syrup, all sorts of things."

"What about meat?"

"I get that canned, too. The pressed meats can be a little salty, though..."

"But they have so many chemicals and preservatives, it can't be good for you to eat only that."

"The preservatives might be my problem..."

That's when Guy arrived, armed and bareheaded, one cheek smeared with some sort of grease, handsome as saviours always are. For the first time, I noticed the little flecks of silver sprinkled throughout his mop of hair. Like Madeleine, we'd all end up bleached of colour, canned pea–eating ghosts. But, despite everything— against the antiquated decor that reeked of ammonia, home to mangy (and no doubt disease-ridden) cats— he dazzled. Kiss. Tongues. Now. It didn't matter how. Claudine was right. But what if he had someone in his life... what if the attraction wasn't mutual, what about the carpet and everything else...

We moved the buffet to the centre of the room. Guy attacked the carpet, panting and planting his knee on the ground, right into the grimy gravy that time had deposited between each of its natural fibres. We managed to lift the back edge and twist it in a way that would eventually allow us, while skilfully manoeuvring our arms and legs, to roll it up. We had to do so an inch at a time, holding the stinking roll in place while avoiding the cats playing King of the Mountain. Then we carefully placed the furniture back onto the parts of the floor that, little by little, were laid bare. I swallowed the disdain of a middle-class, middle-aged woman addicted to antibacterial lotion and threw all of my strength into the task in an attempt to convince my devoted prince that, despite the repeated offers he'd made since we started struggling under the weight of the carpet, there was no need to run and find extra manpower. I felt that making a man of myself, to use that awful expression, was for the time being the best chance I had of showing off. As long as I could endure the smell.

Armed with a giant coil of rope Guy had had the foresight to bring, we managed to tie up, like a big, filthy brioche, the woolly monster that had been collecting excrement from the surrounding wildlife for more than a half century. Ancient colonies of dust mites were trapped in a labyrinth that would soon be roasted in the belly of a municipal incinerator, and I delighted in their imminent demise as they embarked on a futile migration toward the roll's extremities. We'd have needed huge plastic bags to contain them all. Meanwhile, the cats were sniffing the odours the pipeline of urine and parasites exhaled.

"Good news!" said Guy. "Your floor's not in bad shape. With a little sanding, we could fix it up nicely. But I see some water damage over there, you should find out where it's coming from."

"The window. I used to keep it open for the cats,

but I managed to close it at the end of last winter."

"At the end of winter?"

"Once it thawed."

"You have no one to help you with the house, ma'am?"

"Everyone is dead. I do the best I can. As long as the walls hold up."

"Well. I'll be back soon with a couple of my guys and we'll get this out of here. It's going straight into the Dumpster. I'll put you in touch with someone who can help with the floor."

"You don't do floors?"

"Unfortunately not."

"Too bad."

"I have enough on my plate with the renovations next door."

"And look at me, holding you up."

"It's no trouble, ma'am. I can be here when the floor guy comes, too, if you'd like."

No crazier than the next person, I pounced on the suggestion that hadn't included me.

"Good idea! I can come, too. That way you'll have double the help. And we can see whether there's any other urgent work that needs doing."

The woman lifted her cold, dry hands and placed them on my cheeks, still damp with sweat. Her lips formed a kiss that would have landed on my forehead if I'd been smart enough to bend down. We must have looked like a pair of apricots: one juicy, one dried.

"Oh! My angels, I should have come to you a long time ago. You can always find good people in a school. Now I can die in peace."

Out of the right-hand corner of my eye, I noticed a small, quivering beige spot: a baby cat.

"My God! There are kittens?"

"Caramel had three, but she'll claw your eyes out if you try to touch them. I've given her the back room. We have a kind of understanding: she protects me from thieves, and I leave her alone. There's nothing as vicious as a mama cat."

A large, bushy head appeared above the kitten, its eyes casting a murderous glare. The cat held itself like a cornered panther. A long *hsssssss* escaped a mouth framed by frightening canines, which it then planted in the scruff of its offspring's neck, shuttling it back to the family fold. The kitten curled into a ball like a hairy snail and let itself be carried off without complaint.

"You may need someone to come over to see about the cats, it's a lot for you to handle."

"I don't want them put down."

"We might be able to treat them and find other homes for them."

"Oh, child, nobody wants an old crippled fleabag except an ancient fool like me."

"I adopted an old crippled fleabag," I said. "He only has three legs."

"You're an angel. That's different."

The afternoon's adventures had worn Madeleine out completely. Guy and I left together, leaving her to nap. The guys would pick up the roll of carpet from the balcony once they handed off their hammers to the night crew at the end of their shift. Madeleine had insisted on paying, and we had accepted her twenty-dollar bill, promising to split it between us.

Side by side in the crisp early-autumn air, our noses were still assaulted by the smell of cat piss. It was even worse for Guy, as he'd practically lain down on the carpet in order to pull it up. He walked holding his flannel jacket at arm's length so as not to contaminate it. I talked to fill the silence.

"I'll try to reach social services. Someone needs to come by and check on her every once in a while. We didn't see the whole house, but I doubt the other rooms are any better."

"And someone needs to take care of those cats."

"I have a few contacts, I'll make some calls."

"I'm so used to being covered in grime that I almost never say this, but I'd love a shower right about now. Stale cat piss is a little too much for me."

A shower. Of all the unbelievable scenarios I'd concocted over the past few days in order to end up in

Guy's arms, it had never occurred to me to include a shower scene. In one scenario I was hit by a two-by-four and fainted; in another I saved a worker who'd been impaled by keeping him alive with mouth-to-mouth, leaving Guy grateful — and smitten. In yet another I rushed a child from a burning building at the last minute and Guy resuscitated *me* with mouth-to-mouth. But I'd completely overlooked the banal efficiency of a plain old shower and the fabulous series of happy events that can result from water cascading over bodies. In times of war, love is fuelled by tragedy; in times of peace, by soap. Everyone knows that. Even though I hadn't thought of it before, I ran with the idea.

"I live two blocks away. I have a nice big shower and it's brand new . . . plus, I have soap and a washing machine." (And white wine in the fridge — I loved where this was going. Brilliant, Diane!)

"I've already been gone a while, but hang on a sec, I'll see if Phil can handle another fifteen minutes or so."

He walked away to make his call. After a moment of total shock, I couldn't resist sending a message in all caps to my bestie.

> GUY MIGHT COME
> TAKE A SHOWER
> AT MY PLACE!!!

WHAT?????

YOU TWO MADE OUT???

He ran a hand through his hair as he came back toward me.

(Sweet Jesus. Oh my God, *oh my God*...)

"It's all set. They can handle another few minutes. I'm staying on with the second shift later tonight as it is, because we're short-staffed."

My phone would not stop vibrating. I glanced down at it quickly: Claudine was bombarding me with questions, GIFs of screaming girls raising their fists in triumph, and a variety of colourful emojis. I wasn't sure my phone could handle the attention. With the nonchalance of a woman who invites grubby men to take showers at her place every week, I had the presence of mind to add:

"I could do a quick wash for you. I have a new machine..."

"That's so sweet, but I have nothing to change into."

I pictured him in my kitchen, a towel around his waist. God had clearly decided I'd been a good girl.

"You can borrow a bathrobe."

"Ha! There's no way I'd get it to close, Lady..."

And while he laughed at the offer, I typed out a small cry of victory.

SHOWER CONFIRMED!
HEART ATTACK!

The carpenter in Guy immediately noticed my place had been recently renovated, the work tastefully done. In Adèle's words, he was "sharp as hell." He ran his hand over the counters, the panelling, the faucets, and nodded approvingly. Cat-in-the-box was being coy, rubbing up against his calves and swishing his tail playfully. I had to stop myself from saying "Look at Mommy's little cutie!" so Guy wouldn't think solitude had turned me into a crackpot who talks to cats.

He whistled in admiration when he saw the bathroom. I handed him a towel, a washcloth, and a new bar of soap.

"You sure you don't want to go first?"

"No, no, you're on the clock. I don't have to be back until 3:15."

"Okay, I'll be quick."

He pushed the door closed but didn't shut it all the way, and I stood on the marble doorstep, petrified, tracing the veining of the stone with my eyes and wondering whether or not the opening was a metaphor I should take advantage of, a subconscious invitation to seize, or simply a habit without ulterior motive. What with a shower's three-and-a-half minutes limiting my attempts at armchair psychology, I went with the maternal tack more in my wheelhouse.

"Are you hungry?"

"Ah, thanks, but I ate not too long ago."

I remembered Charlotte's advice about details I had to learn to decode. I couldn't pass up the line he'd practically thrown to me.

"You brought your lunch?"

"Yeah."

The question was already so ridiculous, I might as well keep going. Much easier to appear the idiot when you aren't actually locking eyes with the other person.

"Do you make your own lunches?"

"Uh... it depends on the day."

Wrong question, his answer was riddled with holes. It was completely possible that someone else prepared his meals on certain days. Who was it? What did they make? Lasagna? Wild boar? Veggies or no veggies? Construction workers hated vegetables, didn't they? (I had my prejudices, just like the next person.) I was about to ask him why it depended on the day when I stumbled upon my reflection in the hallway mirror and saw the almost half-century written all over my body, from my droopy contours and wrinkled skin to my tired eyelids and cheeks that were beginning to sag. The nervous little girl who, a moment ago, was wondering what to do with the man in her shower had vanished, booted aside by the boring wife Jacques had left in tatters when he ran off one beautiful spring day. Yes, Jacques. It was him, my unfaithful ex-husband, whom I invariably thought of any time I scrutinized myself too closely. Through the filter of his eyes still full of juvenile desire, I appeared faded and out of place. I started to knead my flabby skin, multiplying the craters formed by cellulite and accentuating my fleshy parts, my double chin, my almost liquid that's-its. I needed to see all my unattractive corners, to make myself suffer, and to hurt until I could no longer bear the pain, so that the shipwreck of my life made sense and seemed natural — even deserved. Jacques hadn't looked elsewhere for no reason. I squeezed and prodded, obsessed by my body's biggest flaws and proving to myself that I was solely to blame for my physical decline — that this crazy old woman who'd believed love was enough should have been running, pedalling, pumping, lifting, straining, and sweating...

"'Scuse me, Diane..."

With one set of angry fingers, I was pinching a fold of my belly fat; with the other hand, I was lifting a corner of my shirt to have a better look. When I let go, the fabric remained where it was, outrageously ignoring the laws of gravity. Inviting unspeakable humiliation, I smoothed my top seven or eight times before it fell into place over my stomach. I was so overcome that it took me some time to realize nothing was covering him but the towel and his tattoos. I focused on his eyes so that my own wouldn't stray indelicately and make everything even more awkward, if that were possible.

"Uh..."

Propriety would demand he pretend he'd not seen anything, and that he then add some comment, permitting both of us to act as if he hadn't caught me in blatant self-denigration. But he went where I didn't expect him to go.

"I know it's none of my business, but, ah, I just want to say . . . you're beautiful, Diane."

All the blood rushed back to my head in one swift burst. He raised his hand as if to say, *Okay, I'm going, just forget what I said,* as he darted back toward the bathroom, then thought better of it.

"Know what? I think I'll take you up on your offer. I can't bear to put these clothes back on."

"Okay."

"It'll give me time to make a few phone calls. I've got a bunch of orders to place. As long as that doesn't bother you."

"Of course it doesn't. Quite the opposite."

Which could have been considered inappropriate, given that the opposite was "I'm bothered" — as in, "I'm all hot and bothered knowing that you're sitting half-naked on my couch while I take a shower. I'm 'bothered' because it ignites a thousand hopes within me and revives parts of my body now shuddering with the thrill of it all."

"Give me your clothes," I said.

"No, no, I can take care of it myself, just show me where the machine is."

"Oh goodness, hand them over. I've seen dirty laundry before. Plus, the machine is complicated."

Which was wholly untrue. I was mostly thinking of my not-so-tiny panties in the laundry room, hanging from the bubble-gum-pink circular drying rack I'd bought at Canadian Tire some twenty years ago and can't seem to get rid of. No matter which tangent our story was to take — whether it would remain within the confines of a beige friendship or be engulfed by the flames of an all-consuming passion — there was no way my underwear was making an appearance in the form of a mobile.

Guy pointed at one of the counter stools.

"May I?"

"Sure, go right ahead . . . But wouldn't you be more comfortable on the couch?"

"The towel's damp, I wouldn't want to get your cushions wet."

"Hang on, I'll get you a dry one. Or two."

In the bathroom, I glanced over at the steamed-up mirror and told myself, *You're beautiful, Diane, you're beautiful, Diane*, before going back out.

"Here, this one's bigger, it'll be even better. Put it over the one you're wearing and have a seat."

He went into the bathroom to make the switch. Fine, whatever.

I threw his clothes into the machine without emptying the pockets first (I didn't want an old Kleenex to kill the moment) and caught a glimpse of the waistband of his boxer briefs: a store-brand knockoff. Jacques would never have worn store-brand underwear; he was too invested in the name-dropping that was his mother's legacy and that he applied even to his choice of undergarments. I glanced at the bottle of vanilla-scented fabric softener before deciding against it: a few drops of a misleading scent might wreak havoc on his life, and for now his only crime was an aversion to old cat piss.

"It's my turn, I'm hopping in the shower. You can grab anything out of the fridge if you'd like."

"I'll take a glass of water."

"Above the sink!"

I scooped up my phone and ducked into the bathroom. I switched on the fan and opened the tap all the way, teenager that I was.

"I don't know what to do! I still don't know if he's single."

"Oh, come on! He takes a shower at your place, he tells you you're beautiful, and he's half-naked in your living room. What else do you need..."

"He's wearing a towel."

"A towel? Might as well be a damn fig leaf! And you think he has someone waiting at home?"

"He wouldn't be the first."

"He doesn't seem like that kind of guy."

"We don't know that."

"THEN ASK HIM, FOR GOD'S SAKE! Don't you dare pass up the chance of a lifetime because you're too afraid to ask!"

"But I can't ask him *now*—he's in a towel! It would come across as an invitation to jump into bed with me."

"You can do it on the couch."

"I haven't even shaved!"

"What are you waiting for? Hang up and go shave!"

"I'm too nervous, I'll cut myself. And if he sees that I'm bleeding, he'll know I just shaved and I'll look like that girl who's too pushy and needy."

"Then don't shave."

"And anyway, I didn't call to talk about shaving—I need some advice: do I bring my clothes into the bathroom and change here, or do I walk out in a towel and get dressed in my room?"

"Well, he thinks you've been in the shower for ten minutes already. He's really gonna think you're weird if you leave now to go get your clothes!"

"Okay, towel it is! I'll change in my room. I'll shave, then walk out in a towel."

"Are we talking your legs or *everything*?"

"You think I'm too old for laser hair removal?"

"Stay focused, Diane."

"He might not even see me since he's in the living room and my bedroom is on the other side."

"Then make some noise when you leave. Drop something."

"Oh, I'm doing laundry! I should check on it."

"Good! Go in your towel."

"You don't think that's coming on too strong? I walk out in a towel and head straight to the washing machine..."

"HEY! THE GUY'S IN YOUR LIVING ROOM NAKED, HE'S NOT THERE TO EAT MUFFINS, GO!"

She hung up. I walked over to the door and opened it: the only thing I could see was the back of his head, which wasn't moving. He must have been texting. I cocked an ear: the load was done. Back over to the mirror: *You can do this, Diane. Go, go, go!* Into the shower, shave the armpits, the calves, the—no, too sensitive, ah! too bad—ding ding, text from Claudine: screen shot of an old article from *La Presse* entitled "Beware of the Hairless Vagina," clean up any small nicks, wrap the towel around the bust, deep breath, rearrange the hair, hand on the doorknob, another deep breath, grand entrance, head over to the washing machine, new attempt at memorable conversation.

"There are only three pieces, they'll take about fifteen minutes to dry."

It was a domestic remark, sure, but it got me moving and helped me deal with the improbability of the
situation.

"Hmm...? Oh, thanks."

"Oh! Were you sleeping?"

"Sorry, I dozed off for a bit."

"Don't apologize, you look beat. I should have let
you sleep."

"Nah, I need to get back soon."

"How's fifteen minutes in the dryer?"

"Sounds great."

As I loaded the clothes in, I spied a corner of the
twenty-dollar bill Madeleine had given us peeking out
of a pocket. I walked back over to him, trying to make
light of my indecent attire.

"Look, even our twenty bucks will be clean. I'll put
it in the sun so it dries."

Empty glass of water in hand, he walked over to
me as I took almost laughable care to smooth the bill,
passing my fingers over the everlasting sovereign's old
granny face. When his arm touched mine, an electric
shock shot across my skin.

"Sorry!"

"No! It's me, I drag my feet too much."

I tried to swallow, but there wasn't a molecule of

saliva left in my mouth. He placed his huge calloused paw on my arm—slowly, so I had time to see it coming.

"I have an idea," he said.

"Oh?"

"Let's buy ourselves drinks with all that cash."

I needed Claudine to tell me if this was a date. We were like two kids who'd found a pack of gum still in the wrapper.

"When?"

"Later?"

"I don't get off until six, that must be late for you."

"At this rate, I'll have to stay late, too."

"That's my fault."

"Not at all."

"No one's expecting you at home?"

Knock-knock. Adèle's face was pressed against my kitchen window. I expected her to look away, melt from the awkwardness, and run back downstairs. Instead, she chose to open the door and walk brazenly into my kitchen.

"Rosanne won't go to her doctor's appointment!"

"Hello, Adèle."

"You have to make her go!" she wailed. "She needs an X-ray to see if the bone's healing the right way."

"Don't you knock before walking into people's homes?"

"But I saw you through the window."

"Did you notice that I'm not alone?"

"Hi, I'm Adèle."

"Guy."

·It was pointless; she didn't see the problem. If we could hope for one benefit to come from her unbridled consumption of web and TV series of all kinds, it was that she would learn to understand and interpret certain situations without having experienced them. This meant, for instance, realizing she should not interrupt a couple of adults wearing bath towels and talking to each other just inches apart in a kitchen in the middle of the afternoon.

I formed a straight line with my mouth. "Go back to Rosanne, I'll be right down."

"Well, hurry, because we're going to be late. Paratransit's coming in two minutes. We're on the front porch."

"You don't have school today?"

"I ditched so I could take care of Gran."

"Ditched?"

"Yeah. As in I skipped school, for your information."

Exasperating face, shitty attitude, as irritating as a heel blister. I clenched my fists. She took off while Guy turned his back to stifle his laughter.

"Don't laugh!"

"She sure told you."

"Do you have kids?"

"My daughter's an adult, she's thirty now. But I know the game, played it myself."

"Do you see her often?"

"No, she's in Toronto."

"Ah."

"It's complicated."

I went into my room and dressed in a hurry, making sure to choose my panties wisely in case we got around to using that twenty-dollar bill. If the stars managed to align, then what had been thwarted by the ill-timed arrival of a teenager with still-evolving manners might yet come to pass later on.

Rosanne was sulking in her wheelchair, bundled in a thick blanket. She looked as if she'd just been pulled from a burning building.

"This is important, Rosanne. We have to make sure the ankle is healing right."

"Nothing to do but wait, that's what they said. I don't see how one more photo'll change anything."

"They want to make sure the bone's fusing together and that you don't have any other issues."

"Like what?"

"I don't know. Other issues."

"They just want my money."

"Health care is free, Rosanne."

"Nothing's ever free, poor child."

"If it doesn't heal well, it will cost more later on. No matter who pays."

"I'll be dead later on."

"I think you've got a lot of life left in you."

"Don't scare me."

"Time to go, Rosanne, your ride's here."

The driver had just lit a cigarette and was signalling for us to take our time. The curled ends of his Dalí moustache had caramelized from repeated exposure to smoke. I was sure the skin on his fingers had aged similarly.

"And, besides, they take me for a fool! Like I'm three years old. You should hear the way they talk."

"It only seems that way because they speak loudly, they want to make sure you hear. IF I TALKED LIKE THIS, ROSANNE, YOU MIGHT THINK I TOOK YOU FOR A FOOL, BUT MAYBE I JUST WANT TO MAKE SURE YOU HEAR ME."

"True, old people are hard of hearing."

"That's why our ears never stop growing."

"Oh yeah?"

"They act as trumpets, apparently."

"My God! You called me a personal nurse..."

I followed her eyes to see what had just appeared behind me, since sections of wall do not move very subtly. Adèle felt it necessary to make the introductions with a defiant little pout.

"That's not a nurse, Gran. That's her boyfriend, Guy."

"Ah!"

"Oh stop, Adèle, it's not like that!"

"Oh no? So you take showers with your friends now?"

Rosanne didn't react; in fact, she seemed mesmerized. If I'd been an octopus, one of my tentacles would, in a fraction of a second, have shot out to: a) slap Adèle across the face; b) strangle her; c) trip her, making her fall and break her tailbone for good; d) grab her by the waist and throw her across the street and into the tiny puddle of stagnant water Mrs. Dorion was pretending was the Trevi Fountain; or e) all of the above. And since Guy was dressed in his still-damp clothing, he'd presumably seen my underwear mobile. My mind's tentacles were seething.

As I was collecting myself, Guy carried Rosanne down the stairs so she wouldn't have to drag her boot. Adèle, darling child who may have felt the sting of my claws despite her veneer of impertinence, hurried after them with the wheelchair. It was a relief to be forgotten for a moment. I swear I could hear Rosanne purring as the van whisked her away. Guy bent and kissed my hand, then left for the school.

"See you later, Lady Di."

Adèle had ruined our love scene, but that did not diminish my euphoria at the suggestion of a drink. I bounded up the stairs two by two and went over to worship the twenty-dollar bill drying beside the window. I was far too happy for one person.

"You won't believe me."

"You finally had sex!"

"He asked me out for a drink!"

"After you had sex?"

"We didn't."

"WHY NOT?"

*Don't rat on Adèle.* I wanted her death to remain the brief fantasy it was.

"Because."

"I hope the real answer has nothing to do with the word *hair*."

"He had to get back to work. But it's not over yet, he asked me out for a drink!"

"Then he's single!"

"I guess so."

"He wouldn't have asked you otherwise."

"He has a thirty-year-old daughter."

"That gives us a better idea of his age."

"And it means he was probably married."

"No, all it means is that he's had sex at least once in his life."

"Gaaaahhhh."

"This is good! When's the drink?"

"Later tonight."

"Seriously?"

"The twenty bucks won't even be dry."

"What twenty bucks?"

"It's a long story."

"What're you doing now?"

"Shaving."

The greatest joys in life affect our moods like a new red shirt in a load of whites: they colour everything pink. When I ran into Kathleen, who mentioned that she'd told the principal about the potentially dangerous ball strap we were keeping in our classroom, I smiled and suggested she call the SPCA. Outside it began to pour, prompting an end to the day's hostilities.

As for Devan, who'd let me have it when I suggested he do a puzzle to calm down—he was trying to slice open the bean bag with a Lego sword he'd made (the kid was clearly a genius)—I simply said, "Come get me when it breaks, okay?" He looked at his sword, scanned the room for someone else who might scold him, then dropped it and wandered over to the reading corner, where he stuck his nose in a pile of books. I said thank you to Éléonore when she pointed out my wrinkles ("What are all those lines?"), counted cards with Julia a dozen times (sixteen in total, I can confirm), and had a ridiculous conversation with Pavel, using my own invented language.

"What are you drawing, Pavel? Ah! It's a house on fire..."

(Shaking his head *No, no, no.*)

"With flowers . . ."

(*Noooo!*)

". . . with scribblydoos . . ."

(Amazement in his eyes. *Yes!*)

"And that's a cow."

(*Noooo.*)

"Oh excuse me, a permiflette."

(*Yes!*)

"Eating a bloody craspiton."

(*Yes!*)

"In a florinny trouk pitouka."

(*Yesss!*)

Revelation! He didn't speak because he couldn't get the words out: their dull and dreary sounds were crippled by boredom as they tried to scale his vocal cords. My diagnosis as amateur shrink: lack of imagination.

And when I managed to secure five minutes to use the bathroom, I screamed, "I'm dooone!" at the top of my lungs after I'd finished peeing. Let them hear me all the way in Australia. I was laughing so hard by the time Linda came in to check on me, she didn't believe me when I said I hadn't smoked a thing.

I answered the phone with this same feverish energy, even though I didn't recognize the number on the screen.

"Hello hello!"

"Yes, hello . . . am I speaking to Diane Delaunais?"

"Yes, this is she!"

"Hello. I'm here with Mr. Valois—"

"Jacques Valois?"

He hadn't said, "I'm here with the body of Jacques Valois," so there was no reason to panic.

"Yes. Mr. Valois has had an accident."

The curtain fell, and the colourful swirls of my inner rainbow vanished on the spot.

"An accident?"

"A cycling accident."

"Cycling?"

"Yes, a rather violent collision."

"With a car?"

"No, actually, it was with, uh…some farm machinery."

"A tractor?"

"Uh…you could say that."

"Where?"

"In Portneuf."

"What was he doing in Portneuf?"

"Cycling."

"Since when does he cycle? He's never cycled before!"

Linda walked over, both hands over her heart, horrified. "Your children?" she mouthed. I shook my head no and closed my eyes. God, no, luckily not my children. She twirled her hand in the air to indicate that she would take over my class. "Take your time," I read on her lips.

"Listen, ma'am, I pulled over as soon as I saw the accident. I was right behind him. I called for help and your husband—"

"*Ex*. My ex-husband."

"Oh! I'm sorry."

"Who asked you to contact me?"

"He did. He gave me your name and number."

"I don't understand, Jacques has a new wife now. We're divorced."

"Look, I'm only trying to help. The paramedics wanted me to contact a member of his family—family or ex-family, I suppose it doesn't matter..."

"So then he was able to speak?"

"A little, once he came to..."

"Did he lose consciousness?"

"Yes, he landed on his head. Cracked the helmet. The paramedic said it saved his life, that he'd be dead otherwise."

"My God..."

"He broke his fall with one hand. Which definitely minimized the impact, but now his wrist isn't bending in the right direction. He must have been going very fast."

"Can he walk?"

"Uh...not at the moment. They've immobilized him from head to toe, they don't want him to move in case he injures something else. Apparently that happens sometimes, even afterwards."

"Which hospital?"

The journey over felt endless, and I had time to convince myself, through a thousand twisted arguments, that all of the misfortunes I'd wished on Jacques since he left me had materialized into one compact mass in the form of a tractor. To punish myself, as I often do when I feel guilty, I committed to a string of promises straight out of a drunkard's playbook.

"If Jacques makes it through without ending up a vegetable, I'll start running, I'll give up eating butter, I'll be super-sweet to Bimbo. If Jacques can just lead some semblance of a normal life, I..."

And I forgot about Guy.

# 9

## In which I look after the feet
## of my idiot ex-husband

All hospitals are alike. They have the same cracked beige walls, the same notice boards overloaded with information supplemented by loose pages affixed with sticky tack here and there, the same poor wretches wandering around flanked by an IV pole, the same medical staff rushing about in coloured scrubs or lab coats and stethoscopes, the same patient codes spat out over medieval intercoms, the same grieving families clutching flowers and stuffed animals, the same uncomfortable chairs discouraging long stays, the same elderly volunteers eagerly directing you to the proper hallways and elevators, the same receptionists tired of repeating that no, they can't predict how long the wait will be.

"I'm looking for someone who just arrived in an ambulance."

"Go to the ER, miss."

"I was told he was here."

"Name?"

"Whichever receptionist was working the ER…"

"Patient's name."

"Oh, uh…Jacques Valois."

"Is that with an *s*?"

"Yes."

"It's so strange how some names end in *s*. Jacques, Georges…I wouldn't put an *s* on Elise, otherwise people might pronounce it *Elisesse*…Spanish speakers would, at any rate. They pronounce all the letters… Okay, hang on, Jacques Valois…he just got out of Radiology, door 8, but they'll have to park him in the ICU since we're full up. No vacancy."

She didn't laugh as she said it; the joke was so old and overused that she'd forgotten it had ever been funny.

The first thing I saw through the small opening in the curtain was his calves, streaked with big blue veins. The paleness of his skin exposed subtle discolorations that would soon reveal themselves for what they were: age spots. At the end of an arm pierced with tubes, an inanimate hand rested on the sheet. His beautiful greying head, immobilized in a plastic vise, was covered in bandages. *It's over*, I thought; this man I had loved, cared for, cried over, would never be able to use his body to love again—not me, not Someone Else, nobody. Lying there helplessly in a poorly tied blue hospital gown, he waited for science to decide his fate and read his sentence. Whatever had remained of my hate after the trip to the hospital flew right out the window. Buoyed by the surf of our old love, which had begun to lift me, I went over to dock gently against the rail of his bed.

"Hey!"

"Diane . . ."

"So this is how you get me to see you?"

"I'm glad you came."

His left hand and forearm were bandaged and held in a sling. What little skin I could see appeared swollen, puffy. A warm, liquid feeling pierced my stomach and my legs felt heavy.

"What have they said so far?"

"Not much, it's still unclear."

"You can move your hand! That's good!"

"This one, yeah. I can't feel the other one. They gave me a shot before they repositioned my wrist. I didn't watch."

"What about your feet?"

"I can feel them. I can even move them, look."

"Your back?"

"They just told me everything looks good. Now they need to check my neck."

I felt a hundred pounds leave me all at once. Sudden weight loss like that can only happen in your head.

"Since when do you cycle?"

"Since I bought myself a bike."

"Along with the cycling shorts, the tight-fitting jersey, the clip-on shoes, and all?"

"Yes, ma'am."

"I won't even ask how much it cost."

"I wanted to get back into shape."

"You could just run around the neighbourhood like everyone else. All you need is shoes — plus, no tractors."

"They took off my socks. I hate having bare feet."

"I can get you another blanket."

"Thanks. I'd rather have socks, but oh well."

"I don't have socks."

"They won't take this damn brace off. And I'm not allowed to get up."

"What about going to the bathroom?"

"I call the nurse and he helps. It's great for bladder control, let me tell you."

I thought to myself, *And what if he becomes a she?* Now that I knew his extremities hadn't lost all sensation — the soft tissue as well, I had no doubt — reality set back in and the pawns resumed their positions. The pain and pity that had, only moments ago, made me forget I was a fallen woman now gave way to a sour taste as I pictured my ex and his bitch locked in a steamy embrace.

The haunting images I had managed to keep at bay for so long were threatening to overpower me.

"Where's Charlene?"

"Ah, Charlene . . . things are a little complicated with Charlene these days."

So that's why I had been called—me, the time-worn boring wife. I thought it might do me good to pour salt on an open wound.

"Complicated?"

"The birth was tough on Charlene, really tough. Physically, mentally . . . nothing went as planned for her . . ."

Which, in my opinion, should be the one thing taught during prenatal classes: nothing ever goes as planned, or so little that "nothing" is pretty well accurate. You learn to pant like a dog, the nurse asks you to be a snake. You learn how to push during contractions, you're told to wait until a doctor is available. You want a water birth, but none of the tubs are free and the anaesthetist can't come, at least not right away, maybe later, maybe never. You can't manage to get down on all fours or to sing as you'd pictured yourself doing. The atmosphere is nothing like you'd imagined, you hurl insults at all of the people around you who aren't suffering, and you howl, defecate, tear, and try to kill the person alongside you between contractions, just like in the nightmares you didn't dare entertain, your head so stuffed full of the cute scenes you needed to believe in because the only real and honest thing these courses offer is the illusion of control. It works as a natural Ativan to help manage pre-delivery stress, which is completely fair and square.

So when Jacques said that nothing had gone as planned "for her," what I heard was that it had gone well for me—as if the torrent of stretch marks rippling across my stomach and thighs counted for nothing, as if the struggles of his porcelain Thing erased the enormity of what we'd been through together—*three* times instead of once, might I add—experiences that should at the very least remain as etched into his memory as they were on my body.

This is why I had to stop seeing Jacques: my mind reeled at the slightest allusion that devalued me. It was all tremendously unhealthy. I lost so many neurons I would have preferred to destroy in another manner— with white wine, for instance.

"And there's just no end to it. The baby doesn't sleep through the night, Charlene's... well, we think... okay, *I* think... she's a little postpartum. Motherhood has meant giving up so much, in all aspects of her life..."

I didn't give a rat's ass about how Sissypants felt after losing her firm little tummy and the honeyed sweetness of her nights. In fact, it gave me a little thrill to hear she was on the road to premature ageing. The only reason I kept listening to Jacques was because he might have broken his neck.

"It's not her fault, she isn't strong like you, Diane... You didn't even have family to lean on... you were so strong..."

"But boring..."

"No, stop. That's not true."

It felt like opening a beer fridge in the middle of a heat wave and letting the cool breeze lick your neck.

"Your words, not mine."

"Diane..."

His eyes became misty; it was either emotion or the hospital's fluorescent lighting. I clung to my animosity so I wouldn't turn soft and fall apart.

"I think that over time, I ended up confusing some things."

"It's age, Grandpa."

"Maybe..."

"You lost interest."

"I guess stability does that. Along with balance, consistency..."

"*Pfff.*"

"That's what it takes to raise stable kids."

"So they say."

"And that's what we did, we raised three beautiful, stable kids."

"Uh-huh."

"Who are old enough to have kids of their own, I know."

(I faked a smile.)

"When the paramedic asked me who to call, I didn't hesitate for a second."

"That's just habit."

"I don't think so, no."

"You certainly wouldn't have called your mother..."

"I was afraid you wouldn't come. It's crazy, all the things that were going through my mind..."

In the early days after Jacques left, I'd have sold my soul to hear half those words. Now, uttered in a run-down hospital by a bedridden man who had unloved me in a way I never thought possible, they failed to hide the ravaged landscape the hurricane had left in its wake.

"I think I'm an old fool."

"I completely agree."

"Hello! I'm Dr. Morin. Are you the spouse?"

She didn't extend a hand. Not enough time and too many germs.

"No."

"My colleague and I just took a look at the X-rays, Mr. Valois..."

She spoke A LITTLE LOUDLY, which made me smile.

"Would you prefer we spoke in private?"

"It's okay, this is my ex-wife. Do you think you could remove the brace? It's horribly uncomfortable."

"No. Unfortunately, I have some bad news."

"Ah…"

"You've fractured your C4-C5-C6 vertebrae, and you'll need to stay completely immobilized for the moment. The injury may take weeks or even months to heal. You'll likely make a full recovery, but for now it's quite important…"

No introduction, no hesitation, only the facts, dry as unbuttered toast. Back when the children were little, I must have issued a hundred "You're going to break your neck!"s, never thinking any of them would literally break their neck. It's a vague injury that usually requires clarification—you could easily say so-and-so broke his neck and mean that he fractured his ankle. Dr. Morin looked down and checked the pager clipped to her waist.

"I have an ambulance arriving; I'll be back later. The nurse will check in on you. Call if you need anything."

She left, lab coat blowing in the wind, possibly to greet what remained of a motorcyclist or a day labourer reconfigured by a hand saw. I was stunned. If Jacques hadn't spoken first, I'm not sure I would have found the strength to open my mouth.

"We get what we deserve, eh?"

"You won't be able to move for weeks, Jacques…"

"At least Charlene is in Martinique with her parents."

"What about Terrence?"

"He's there, too. And so is the nanny."

"How will you manage all alone?"

"I'll hire someone."

"Ah! Some young nurse..."

He didn't seem to catch the jibe. It was dumb, anyway.

"Can you hand me the button? I can't find it any-where."

"What's wrong?"

"I need to pee. My bladder's about to explode."

When the nurse came, I pretended I'd left my phone in the car in order to give them a moment. Jacques believed me, of course, but the nurse gave me a subtle wink.

I stopped in front of the gift shop, where an epidemic of smiley faces was raging. A woman plugged into some sort of artificial respirator was thumbing her yellowed hands through religious cards embellished with gold glitter, a good reminder of Church-mandated poverty. I caught a glimpse of myself in the oval mirror sitting beside the display of reading glasses: face like a dead fish, eyes ringed with large purple circles that drooped down like soft, almost creamy moons. Upstairs, Jacques was waiting for me with his strange confusion and repentance, both of which were useless to me. It's easy to blame yourself once the battle's been waged, the war is over, and it's time to count the bodies. Easy to make me falter—me, the boring wife abandoned among the corpses, my tattered love left dangling but still searching for purchase despite it all.

He'd exposed his doubts and existential troubles to me out of sheer cowardice, now that there was no going back. I should have returned to his room and told him just where to go, told him that I was about to jump into bed with a man built like a tank who'd fuck me in every position imaginable because I was done being so goddamn faithful. Instead, I bought a pair of socks with reinforced heels and marched back to the ICU to spruce him up. Like a fool.

I'd written to Charlotte earlier, and she had left a message: of course, she'd be happy to go by Madeleine's and take a look at the cats. She would talk to Dominic, her big-hearted animal saviour, and he'd pick up the ones needing to be transported or relocated — as in "put down or given away." I wanted to call her back to say that her father had just broken his neck, but I would have had a hard time explaining why I was here at the hospital. And, besides, it was up to Jacques to decide when and how he wanted to break the news.

Meanwhile, Claudine had bombarded my phone with text messages. She wanted to know where and when I was meeting Guy, what I was planning to wear, and all the rest. I couldn't help firing off a response.

You won't believe this,
but it is what it is:

> I'm at the hospital
> with my old fool of
> an ex-husband, who
> just broke his neck.
> I'm not kidding.
> No Guy tonight.
> I'll explain later.

I hit "send" and then powered down. I could almost feel Claudine's screams through the hand that had closed around my now-paralyzed phone.

"You found socks?"

"In the gift shop. There's a lingerie section. I also bought you a surprise."

"Oh?"

I held out the smiley stress ball like a Lotto winner.

"Oh!"

"For your good hand. You can switch between calling the nurse and squeezing the ball."

"That was sweet of you."

"Does it hurt?"

"This damned brace is going to drive me crazy."

"Will you have to keep it on the entire time?"

"Not this one, they'll give me another. One with a little more padding, apparently."

"It's going to feel like a long, long time."

"I'll ask them to give me something so I can sleep through the next two months."

"Hello again, you two!"

The doctor was back again, her lab coat fluttering like a cape behind her.

"Mr. Valois...I have some good news!"

"Better than last time?"

"Listen to this: I just spoke to the radiologist..."

"Uh-huh..."

"Those aren't fractures in your neck, it's osteoarthritis. It's a severe case, but that's all it is."

She stood still and let the words sink in, as proud as if she'd just invented the wheel. It was the first time I'd seen someone so delighted to be wrong.

"What do you mean? Are you sure? Just a few minutes ago..."

"Our ER machines aren't that accurate, but the ones in Radiology work wonders. And of course, we aren't radiologists..."

"So what happens now?"

"We'll remove the neck brace and give you a temporary splint for your wrist. Then we'll check your other injuries and give you an outpatient appointment with orthopedics. Things will move fast, since we'll probably have to operate. You'll be followed by an occupational therapist afterwards, but you'll be able to sleep in your own home. What do you think—do you like that ending better?"

There was a hint of sea salt on the ends of her vowels, a touch of New Brunswick, perhaps.

"What about the osteoarthritis?"

"There isn't much that can be done, everyone has it. It's a very common type of bone disease that affects everyone differently. You can do PT to strengthen your muscles, or we can send you to rehab and they can give you cortisone injections for pain relief. Did your neck bother you at all before the accident?"

"Not really. I woke up stiff every now and then, like everyone else."

"You're going to have more stiffness now because of the accident, but I don't think it'll be any worse than that. Always wear a helmet, that's very important. Don't stop cycling, the exercise is good for your heart. And try to avoid machines, as my grandmother would say."

She gave his arm a gentle squeeze on her way out, a kind of goodbye she must have developed from treating patients in poor shape or who had no hands. I had just lost a few more pounds. I'd end up a skeleton after all these hospital visits.

The kind nurse appeared as if he'd been waiting behind the curtain the entire time.

"Hey! I hear you're busting outta here! It's a good thing, too, because we need the bed. We just had a couple of guys arrive who are real banged up. Fell three floors down; the porch railing broke. Can you believe it? You're at home takin' it nice and easy, you're out gettin' some fresh air, and *bam*, railing breaks right out from under you! One has a perforated lung and a fractured pelvis, fell right onto a concrete wall. The other guy got away with a broken arm and bruises on one side of his head. Looks like he dove headfirst, but he's still better off than this fella I had the other day…"

As he worked to release Jacques, anaesthetizing him with tales of dislocated parts and dismembered bodies (how can you complain about a neck brace when you hear about a leg caught in a metal shredder?), I watched the scene play out like it was theatre. Once he was on his feet, the bandages unwrapped—"They're just surface wounds, we'll disinfect them and let 'em breathe"— Jacques straightened up and reclaimed his status as a man of the world who'd been offered a second chance at life, away from me and the older children who'd refused to be their new brother's godparents. They'd punished him for my sake, I thought. One day I hoped they would come to love the little terror, but for the time being everyone was still licking their wounds.

Blue hospital gown and splint on his wrist aside, the man who'd thrown my life into a tailspin with his sudden burst of hormones stood before me, alive and well. Already, the doubts that had assailed him only hours earlier appeared to have dissipated. Maybe I'd been dreaming. My boundless naïveté depressed me. I had to get the hell out of there.

"You're leaving?"

"Uh-huh."

"You...I...could you take me home?"

I shook my head no.

"But I don't have any clothes."

"Call your sister. You can borrow some of her husband's things."

"Jacinthe? You know I can't say the word *hospital* on the phone or she'll faint."

"Then go to the gift shop. They sell fleece track suits with smiley faces on them. Taxis take credit cards."

"Are you serious?"

I let out a pseudo-natural laugh to give him false hope, as if I were kidding—like in gangster movies when the bad guy announces the torture is over as he's pulling out the handsaw. Except that as I chuckled, I turned around and made an honest-to-goodness break for it. I bet he'd stay there, dumbfounded, for several minutes, maybe even an hour, waiting for me to return before realizing that I'd truly gone. I followed all the official and handwritten Exit signs without stopping until I reached the right door. An old man was sleeping in one of the waiting rooms I passed through, fists tucked under his arms, chin planted on his enormous

Adam's apple. I swerved toward him, tripping over his outstretched legs blocking the way.

"Move your legs! This isn't a dormitory!"

It was nothing personal; I needed to find an outlet for my dark mood.

In the car, I cried calmly. No sobbing, no shouting. My first tear traced a path that others followed in their own time. I waited for them to dry and leave salt marks, then swept these away with the back of my hand. I felt a detachment I didn't recognize.

When I arrived home, I took out three trinkets I'd bought for the purpose (a ghastly snake vase, an Easter bunny that looked more like an egg, and something abstract that made me want to puke), lined them up on a huge wooden cutting board, and smashed them to bits with my sledgehammer. I would likely find pieces under the furniture for months, and it would be impossible to tell what belonged to which sacrifice. That is the beauty of ugliness.

I went down to join Claudine, who was waiting for me with an I'll-try-not-to-ask-questions-but face.

"I guess it's too late to call Guy."

"I don't even have his number."

"We found the *Titanic*, I'm sure you could figure it out."

"I don't know his last name."

"We can look on Facebook, he might have posted a picture."

"There must be a hundred thousand Guys."

"No, only old men are called Guy. Nobody names kids that these days, thank God."

She handed me a glass of white.

"Here, listen to the voice of Riesling."

That always amused us. Life is complicated, but we are easily entertained and there's solace in that.

"He thought his neck was broken."

"Bungee-jumping?"

"Cycling."

"Jacques rides a bike?"

"Sure does."

"What did you do at the hospital?"

"Torture myself."

"Oh stop..."

"And buy socks."

"Him and his goddamn feet..."

"But in the end, it turns out he's just old. He has a bad case of arthritis."

"Hah! The old goat! Sorry he doesn't have it somewhere else, if you ask me."

"You need a bone to have arthritis."

"I know, life isn't fair."

And we decided, over a large and horrifyingly meaty

cassoulet at the bistro, that what mattered lay ahead, and that somewhere in this future existed a handsome man with a terrible name who would be good company for the chilly fall evenings.

"And the next time you go running to that idiot's bedside like the imbecile you are, I swear I'm going to bust through the wall of your old house — with a bazooka, if I have to — and bring you the envelope hiding all his little secrets. I'll tie you to a chair and read what it says, line by line, until your nose bleeds."

I hadn't read a word of the report from the detective I'd hired after Jacques left me. In a moment of lucidity, I'd stuffed it into the hole I'd "accidentally" put through the wall of my living room to be sure I'd never lay my hands on it again. A contractor had come by to seal the opening, eliminating all possibility of Knowing. Jacques had ruined our future. I couldn't run the risk he'd tarnish our past.

"Tomorrow's Saturday. We're going shopping for lingerie. You'll need a new erotic identity."

"*Nooo*! You've been reading old-lady magazines again!"

"When you go on that date with Guy —"

"If it ever happens."

"— you can't wear big granny panties."

"No."

"You wear your prettiest pair."

"Makes sense."

"And your prettiest pair, since I doubt you've bought anything new since that asshole left—"

"You don't know that!"

"—you'd have told me otherwise—must be the pair Jacques liked the most?"

"..."

"Well there you go, enough said."

I *was* in need of a new identity, erotic or otherwise. Sometimes scissors work as well as a sledgehammer.

# 10

## In which we tighten our ranks
## and our bra straps

'll never understand through what black magic harsh fitting-room lights so cruelly destroy the illusions filling our heads, those ridiculous amalgamations inordinately fuelled by images of the sickly thin and disturbingly young. They're as ridiculous as they are treacherous.

"Let me see!"

"No. I look like a sausage."

"Oh stop, it looks great!"

"On the plastic mannequin with the butt of a ten-year-old nymph, it would."

"You said it, the butt of a nymph. In real life, sometimes your ass hangs out a little."

"It looks like I have four ass cheeks!"

"Show me."

"Noooo!"

"This pair's supposed to be like a bandeau."

"A bandeau around all this flab? More like a choker."

"It's too small, that's all."

"No, it won't work."

"Okay, I'll bring you something else."

"Forget it, I've had enough."

"Try the bras while you wait."

Inside the fitting room hung bras of all colours, their embroidered designs shooting me nasty looks. They would be too beautiful, my skin too pale. A homemade cake never looks like the one on a magazine cover. I put on the first bra, making a superhuman effort to avoid looking at myself in the kaleidoscope of mirrors holding me hostage. Then I took a deep breath and looked up: my breasts were running away from each other like angry lovers. The promise of handsome cleavage offered by the buxom mannequin in the window feeding window shoppers' naïveté would never become a reality. My breasts were not about to be magically transformed into a pair of mouth-watering knockers destined to bring men to their knees. I readjusted the straps, played with the inserts, and gave up. My breasts would never be foghorns. Thank goodness. I'd do without, just as I'd done up until now without too much trouble.

"Show me."

I opened the door without a fight. Claudine made a face, took a step back, and tilted her head thirty degrees. The sales assistant walked over, placing her feet delicately onto the worn industrial carpet in front of the mirrors.

"Hang on a minute, I'll tighten the straps . . . Oh! You already have."

She squeezed the sides of my breasts to force them into the cups and see what could be gained by cinching the bra even tighter. I almost bit her.

"You have large breasts. These styles aren't right for you, you need a stronger underwire."

Large breasts. The highlight of my week. Even so, depression won out in the end and I left empty-handed, morale through the floor. The other sales associate, the one who had been making little underwear pyramids on the display in the entryway during my walk of shame, came running up after me on the sidewalk, glasses halfway down her nose. I went through the list: purse, phone, keys . . . I hadn't forgotten anything.

"Miss! Miss! Excuse me . . . you know, other places carry lingerie brands that would fit you wonderfully . . . Sokoloff is really affordable, and you can find them at Simons."

"Brands for fat asses?"

"No, brands for all kinds of *normal* women, miss."

She smiled through clenched teeth before turning

and sailing back toward the boutique like a warm breeze.

"Okaaaaay! I like her!" hooted Claudine. "Simons, let's go!"

"No, I've had enough. I'm done for the day."

"Then what will you wear?"

"It's not going to happen, anyway."

"Hey! You had an official date! If your nut-job ex hadn't suffered an existential crisis after smacking into a tractor, you and Guy would still be in bed."

"It's better this way. Char's coming over soon, and we're going to see Madeleine. That needs taking care of."

"Oh right, because wiping some crazy cat lady's ass is way more fun that screwing a hottie."

"I don't even have his number!"

"Well, you're in luck, because I have another idea! Piece of cake!"

"NO! Thank you. My head's still spinning from the hours of Facebook photos you made me look at."

"You're so boring."

"I'm well aware of it, thanks."

"I don't mean that kind of boring."

"There aren't a hundred ways to be boring."

"Okay, come on. I'll help you make the stew."

"You shouldn't, it's really boring.

"I'll help you if you stop sulking."

"I'm not sulking."

"Making stew can be super-fun."

"No wine before five."

"Killjoy."

"You are!"

"Geez, if I had your luck, I'd buy some stroganoff and dive straight into his bed."


We'd just started peeling root vegetables to the strains of our "old-lady music," as Adèle called it, when she came in to tell us she was going to see a friend.

"Can you give me a ride?"

"No. You have a bus pass, and that's faster than a car anyway."

"Lame."

"You're right. Some people are cool and some are lame, what do you want? I'm lame, deal with it. What's your gran doing?"

"She wants to come up and help."

"No sir, not with that boot. Tell her we'll come to her instead. Hang on, Adèle, help us bring everything down."

"Oh, is that how it is? You won't help me out with a ride, but I'm supposed to help you carry stuff?"

I have rarely seen hackles rise quite so fast.

"WHAT? I don't help you? Of course not! I never do anything for you. I never clean up after you, never shop or make dinner for you, never take care of you, never bring you to the dentist, the doctor, the hairdresser, the beauty salon . . . I spend my time picking up after you, cooking for you, remembering everything you forget, helping you with your homework, smoothing over your little tantrums at school so you don't get kicked out . . . No, I don't spend the whole day bored out of my mind in a shitty office so that I can earn enough money to put a roof over your head, pay the heating and internet bills, afford your braces and those goddamn jeans with holes in them, of course not—"

"Mom—"

"—but I don't help you, *noooo*. I don't do a thing—"

"Mom!" Adèle was standing with her arms crossed, looking amused. "You can flip out so fast."

"Well, think about what you said!"

"I was kidding."

"I don't believe you."

"Tell me what to bring down."

As my friend struggled to recast her face into the picture of a calm mother, I reached into my purse and dug up the fabric patch I'd bought for Adèle at the hospital gift shop. In dazzling gold letters, its consummate kitschy font spelled out *God is Love*. I walked over to the unfortunate teenager, exploited and neglected, removed the protective backing from the patch and, feigning a need to grab the bag of potatoes, furtively stuck it onto the pocket of her backpack as I passed.

Adèle added a scarcely audible "fucking meno-pause," which luckily didn't reach Claudine's ears. But as I'd just—gently, ever so gently—avenged us, it didn't seem fair to overdo it. Instead, I pressed the patch a little harder to make sure the glue would adhere to the backpack permanently.

When Charlotte and her boyfriend arrived, I left Claudine to finish the stew and jumped into the van from the animal shelter. It was even more pungent than I remembered (a clever mix of wet dog, hockey bag, and human corpse). Dominic was exuding his usual laid-back vibe; his attire spoke volumes about his rejection of fashion, as well as the hygienic norms of "all those fanatical anti-germ nut jobs." Even without a microscope, I was able to confirm beyond any reasonable doubt that his own germs were doing just fine. I felt for my daughter.

"Okay, Mom, we have a game plan."

"I'm listening."

"We'll need time to examine the cats without the lady panicking, so we think you should sit with her and talk about the weather or something. Whatever keeps her occupied. It'll be less stressful and help us work better."

"Okay."

"Dom will look over the cats and identify the males and females, figure out how old they are, which ones are sick—"

"What will you do if they are sick?"

The two exchanged a quick glance. Charlotte put her right hand over her left and spread her fingers into a kind of star-shaped buoy, like she did every time she had something serious or difficult to say.

"It depends."

"On what?"

"On how sick the cat is. We'll take the worst cases to the shelter to see what can be done."

"Will you have to kill any of them?"

"Euthanize? Yes, it's possible. We'll try to put as many up for adoption as we can. But let's be honest, people don't like old cats."

"Or old people, for that matter."

"I like old people! Especially old moms..."

She rested her cheeky little head on my shoulder. It's the kind of joke you tolerate when you're on the threshold of a round number, no matter which one.

"Will you save the babies?"

"Who can resist a cute kitten? The problem is that they don't stay cute for long. We just pick them up further down the line."

"I know, sweet pea..."

"While you and Dom are doing that," Charlotte said, "I'll take care of the mom and her babies. That will probably be the hardest part."

"You won't be able to get near her."

"Hah!"

Dominic gave me a wink.

"Your daughter can get near any animal she wants."

"I know."

Madeleine took five interminable minutes to open the door, giving me the time to cook up all sorts of disastrous scenarios that, regardless of how they ended, featured a rotting corpse. But the door did finally open, and there was Madeleine standing in its frame, a fragile rice-paper doll wearing the same clothes as the day before.

"Hello, Madeleine! It's me, Diane. I helped with the carpet yesterday."

"Oh my Lord, you came back!"

"I brought my daughter, Charlotte."

"Oh! What a lovely young woman! My God!"

"Hello, ma'am!"

Madeleine's eyes filled with tears, flooded by long-buried memories and grief that bobbed to the surface. Ammonia had the same affect on me.

"I mentioned her yesterday. My daughter is studying to be a veterinarian."

"Oh yes! What a wonderful job, treating sick animals. You'll earn your place in Heaven, my word..."

"This is Dominic."

"Hi, ma'am!"

"He'll be taking the animals to the shelter. And he's Charlotte's boyfriend."

"Oh! You two are engaged?"

"No, we're not."

"Will the wedding be soon?"

"Uh...no, we have no plans to marry."

"Better to hold off until you really know each other. In my day, these things couldn't wait."

"It's just that we're not interested in getting married," Dominic insisted. "People don't get married all that much anymore, it isn't necessary. A wedding's a big hassle, plus, it's expensive. The whole idea's pretty ridiculous, if you ask me..."

I gave my not-son-in-law's ribs a subtle — yet sharp — jab. Madeleine hardly needed us darkening her mood by explaining that the institutions she had known and respected were shit. She might still hold the belief that children born out of wedlock are bastards and that holy matrimony truly is holy.

"Is this a bad time, Madeleine?"

"No, no, I was just having a snack."

"Dominic and Charlotte have time today to examine the cats, to see how many there are..."

"It's a good idea to count them, but it won't be easy. They're in and out all the time, plus, some of them look a lot alike."

"Shall we come take a peek?"

"Sure, come on in. Best to keep your shoes on, though. And we can share my snack, I always have too much."

A jar of mandarin oranges sat on a plastic mat at the end of the table, a plastic spoon resting beside it in a small pool of syrupy juice. A pair of tabbies were eyeing the spread from a distance while a third cat, so black it looked almost blue, was lazing about on the back of the couch. We suspected that some of the animals had taken refuge under the furniture or fled to dark corners when they heard us coming.

"That's very nice of you, but we've just eaten."

"Yes, we're very full, thanks."

"I wouldn't say no."

My second jab did nothing to discourage Dom, who walked cheerfully over to the table like the simpleton he sometimes is. When Madeleine offered to find him a clean spoon, he took the opportunity to display his sophistication.

"Nah, I'd rather use my fingers."

Not waiting for an invitation, he plunged his mangy-stray-animal-collector's fingers into the jar, grabbed an orange segment, and shoved it crudely into his mouth. Then he licked the syrup as it dribbled down his hand before performing the whole routine again — twice. It was a thing of beauty. Charlotte laughed as if she thought he was cute. I have never understood and probably never will understand her attraction to him, and gave up trying to do so a long time ago. The only plausible explanation I can find is that Dominic is the antithesis of Jacques in all things. When I have a hard time hiding my reservations, I smile and grit my teeth. So I gritted them. But Madeleine was so visibly delighted at the prospect of sharing her "fresh" fruit with someone that I had to admit there were some advantages to his bonhomie and natural non-revulsion.

As Charlotte and her prince charming walked through the house to get a better idea of what the menagerie entailed, I sat down with Madeleine while she finished her snack.

"You have such a beautiful daughter!"

"Thank you. Though sometimes I wonder if she really is mine."

"Why is that?"

"She's so calm, so poised."

"You seem calm to me."

"Bah ... not all the time."

"But that's normal, love."

"Do you know what I do when I lose my cool?"

"You swear?"

"I take a sledgehammer to the furniture and decor. While swearing."

It was the first time she'd opened her eyes wide enough that I could see the whites. She raised a trembling hand to her mouth.

"You destroy the furniture?"

"When my husband left me last spring—"

"Oh no!"

"—I smashed the sofa and the kitchen buffet from my mother-in-law, made a hole in the wall, and even tore out the built-in speakers. Then my therapist suggested I move on to trinkets. They're not as expensive to replace."

"Oh!"

"I shouldn't be telling you this."

"On the contrary!"

"It's just that it helps calm me down."

"It must feel good."

"Very good."

"I might have to try it sometime..."

Charlotte quietly approached and knelt down in front of Madeleine, who was eyeing the furniture around her. I wondered if I might come to regret the conversation we'd just had. A grey cat with a white patch on its neck followed close on her heels.

"Oh hey, big guy, you want some cuddles, don't you?"

"That one is a big ball of mush!"

"How many cats did you start out with, Madeleine?"

"Oh Lord... when I first got here... two."

"And how long ago was that?"

"Oh Lord..."

She looked up at the ceiling as she considered the answer.

"It was the year we were married."

As in "Forever ago."

"I found them at my parents' farm, and I took them in. They'd have died otherwise, the mother didn't want them."

"Oh? Why not?"

"Too scrawny. Nature chooses the strong ones, that's how it is. The mother saves her milk for those with the greatest chances of survival."

"You managed to feed them?"

"That I did. I made a nipple by soaking the corner of a tea towel in warm milk."

"And it worked?"

"Like a charm. We saved a good many cats that way."

"Wow! And how old were you when you moved in?"

"Seventeen."

"Shit, you were still a minor!" The prince slapped his forehead as he walked into the room.

"Yes, the priest granted us a special dispensation so we didn't have to wait as long."

"Oh boy! You were in a real hurry!"

I closed my eyes so I wouldn't see him thrusting his pelvis back and forth.

"If I'd known death would wait, I'd have taken my time."

"What would you have done instead?"

"Oh, so many things..."

"Well, don't worry, you'll die. We can give you a hand if need be."

"Dom!"

"How's it going so far, Char?"

"It's going."

"How are you keeping track?" I asked.

"We're tagging them," Dom said.

"Tagging them?"

"We cut a small tuft of hair from their back. It doesn't bother the cats, and it grows back quickly."

"Oh, I forgot to tell you! Don't go into the back room, Caramel's in there with her babies," Madeleine warned us.

"I already did."

"Lord!"

Charlotte held up a tin of cat food. "Ocean Delights is my magic weapon. It took time, but eventually she came around."

"Oh!"

Charlotte stepped behind Madeleine and gave me a tight smile that said, *It isn't pretty.* Dom opened and closed both his hands twice — at least twenty cats — then turned two thumbs down: not a good situation. We'd suspected as much. Then they returned to their sad task.

"I think we'll need to ... move some of the cats. There are quite a few," I explained.

"Oh? How many?"

"It isn't clear yet."

"I think there are seven or eight."

"There may be more than that."

"You think so?"

"I do. We'll have to close the kitchen window for the winter."

"But the cats need to get out."

"You can keep two or three of the oldest ones that don't need to."

"Where will the others go?"

"To other homes."

"Oh? You think other families will take them?"

"Absolutely. And Dominic will bring them to the shelter, where they'll be cared for until they are placed."

"That would be lovely! Animals are so good for children."

"They are."

She leaned over to me and lowered her voice. "Your daughter looks so much like you."

"You think so?"

"Oh yes ... I had a daughter once, too."

"Oh? I thought you'd only had sons."

"My first child was a girl. I held her in my arms for nine days before I let her go."

"My goodness...I'm so sorry."

"When the doctor broke my water with his long rod, he also broke her back—all along her spine, the poor lamb."

"Oh my!"

"Back then, we were allowed to stay up to nine days in the hospital, and when my time was up, they told me she wouldn't survive. They took her from me. I can still see them wrapping her up."

"Took her where?"

"I didn't ask. Wherever they had to, I imagine. All they said was, 'There's no hope for this child. God is calling her back to Him.' But why send her to us and let her suffer like that, only to call her back right away? I've spent a lifetime wondering, and I still don't understand."

"It was malpractice! You should have pressed charges!"

"Nobody blamed the doctors back then, it just wasn't done—not people like us, anyway. We didn't know a thing about it. She was too weak, they said."

"Madeleine, that's appalling."

"Hate doesn't bring back a child."

"No, it doesn't..."

"I didn't have any other girls. I didn't want any."

I squeezed her hand and tried not to cry. She was looking at me straight in the eyes. Hers were dry, ready to return to dust.

"After that, I started rescuing cats. Especially the weak ones. To get revenge."

"Beats a sledgehammer."

The tabbies had settled down on the table. The more clever of the pair stretched out a paw, dipped it in the syrup, and proceeded to lick its fur and pads like a trained monkey. The other one looked on with confusion, waiting patiently for the syrup to come to it. Cats are as dissimilar as humans.

A little tuft of fur was missing from each of their backs.

"Come to my place for dinner tonight!" I said. "I'm making a stew."

"Oh, a stew! With salt pork?"

"Who makes stew *without* salt pork?"

"They do on TV. I saw it the other day."

"Well, my stew is full of it. My children will be there, and so will my friend Claudine, her daughters, and her mother. Nothing fancy, just a simple meal together."

"That's lovely of you . . . but you've already got quite a crowd."

"We're making enough to feed an army, don't worry."

"I'd rather leave you to your family. These are precious moments."

"Maybe another time?"

"Yes, another time."

Charlotte and Dominic only managed to catch two of the cats, both of them hopeless cases. Dom would return early the following week with reinforcements and extra cages. We decided to try to co-ordinate with Guy so that he could close the window on the same day and prevent other cats from replacing the deportees, and Madeleine agreed to let us contact social services. She had started to feel a little overwhelmed. Coming to the school had been a cry for help.

"These two are quite sick, so we're taking them with us today."

"They are?"

"They're old cats and they need care."

"They don't look sick to me..."

"I know, cats don't complain much. They curl up in a corner when they're in pain. And their fur can throw you off. Look at this one, put your hand here."

"Oh! He's so skinny!"

"His teeth are really bad. He's probably had a tough time eating anything recently."

"I had no idea."

"It's not your fault. With all the cats coming and going, you can't possibly pay attention to what each of them eats. And it's not like he could tell you."

"But still..."

"Madeleine, he's very old. It's normal. No one is blaming you."

205

"How old?"

"Hmm . . . in human years, he must be nearly a hundred."

"Oh!"

"He wouldn't have lived so long without you."

"And you can treat him?"

"We'll do our best."

"Will you bring him back when you're done?"

"Would you like that?"

"Could you place him with a family?"

"If you'd like, I think that would be a good idea."

"He could make some child happy. My boys loved cats."

"Okay, we'll do that."

"It's better for him."

"And for you."

"Maybe, yes."

Once we were in the van, Charlotte took off her kid gloves.

"We won't be able to treat him, it's already too late."

"Then why didn't you say so?"

"If I had, what would it have changed?"

"But you didn't tell Madeleine the truth!"

"The truth is that we really wish we could save him, Mom, but it doesn't work like that. We euthanize cats in much better shape all the time because we can't find anybody to take them. That's the truth. Would you take one?"

"No, I already have Steve. And he's sick."

"Well, there you go!"

"What's wrong with the other one?"

"Heart murmur on both sides. He could wind up paralyzed or die at any moment."

"How do you know?"

"I listened."

She pointed to the stethoscope that was resting underneath her sweater between her breasts. Disillusion was slowly getting the better of her, at times lending a harsh quality to her voice. Her youthful naïveté had been raked over the coals since she'd started university. Rescue was the goal, but too often you had to kill—even when doing so seemed counterintuitive.

"My baby girl…"

I ran my hand down the length of her beautiful spine, straight and intact, which would make her an oak inside and out. A reed-oak that would know how to bend.

# 11

## In which I fall for it
## like a sucker

When I walked into Claudine's kitchen, the only thing left to do was tie the bundle of beans with dental floss. The animal rescuers would return a little later, once they had done their level best to help the doomed felines. I had invited everyone for six; Alexandre and Justin would arrive right on time as usual, and Antoine and Malika would show up whenever they could. Rosanne was taking a nap after her shift as project manager and foreman of the stew-making site. We'd all eat together to give Rosanne a chance to see everyone, but for now Claudine and I were alone, and I took the opportunity to tell her Madeleine's story. For once in her life, she had nothing to say.

In silence, we sipped a glass of Pinot Gris — the rule of three allowed it — which paired beautifully with our mood but very poorly with the stew. There was almost zero chance the bottle would survive the half hour. We spent a moment lost in thought, savouring our era of failures, melting icebergs, and buffoonish presidents, but also some excellent obstetricians.

"I only have mint-flavoured floss," Claudine pointed out.

"Yuck!"

"You can't taste it."

"Of course you can. You said the same thing about those damned club-sandwich toothpicks last time. I have some of the unflavoured kind upstairs, I'll go grab them."

There on my kitchen table, big red letters scrawled across a sheet of loose-leaf spelled out "GUY," followed by a telephone number. My first text message went downstairs.

> You do have
> unflavoured floss!

I needed a way
to get you upstairs.

> Where did you find it?

On the big sign
in front of the school.

You went to the school?

Char took a picture of
the sign when you went to
Madeleine's. I told her we
wanted to do some work
to the house.

Char knows about Guy.

Call him!!!

He's going to think
I'm a pain in the ass.

He asked you out first.

The shower was my idea.

The drink was his. At the
very least, text him to
apologize for yesterday.
It'll get the ball rolling.

What if he doesn't answer?

You shrug and move on.
And you come finish
your wine.

You won't find anyone more down to earth than
Claudine. I drafted a text message that stuck to the
facts: "Hello! I'm sorry about yesterday, there was an
emergency and I had to rush to the hospital. Let's get
that drink sometime. Diane. xxx" At the last second, I
erased the "x"s. I couldn't judge what degree of intimacy

211

the previous day's shower scene had afforded me. I hit "send" on the way downstairs.

"What's that face for?"

"He already answered!"

"What did you write?"

"What you told me to."

"And what did he say?"

"I don't know, I haven't looked yet."

"It might not even be him."

"It beeped right after I hit 'send.'"

"Look!"

"No."

"Give me your phone."

"No."

"Hand it over! Okay, let's see —"

"What if it's not good?"

"Stop jumping to conclusions! You're driving yourself crazy for no reason! Hang on, I'll read it... Whoa, it's short: 'Are you hurt???' Jesus, what did you write? Come on, Diane, what were you thinking? He's obviously going to freak out if you say you went to the hospital."

"I didn't expect him to think that —"

"Hello! Earth to Diane! 'There was an emergency and I had to rush to the hospital.' What's he supposed to think?"

I desperately missed the days when live conversations

nipped misunderstandings in the bud — when it took three minutes to settle what today requires ninety-seven text messages — many of which are impossible to decode.

"Afterwards I mentioned going for that drink. I think it's obvious I'm not dead."

"Okay then, write back."

"What do I say?"

"Tell him you went for a girlfriend."

"You?"

"Possibly."

"But he's the one who brought us to the hospital after the *Flashdance* episode. He'll think you're doing it on purpose."

"Just tell him it wasn't you, and everything's fine. It's not like he'll ask you who it was."

"You write it, you're better at these things."

"Okay."

"What're you going to say?"

"What I just told you."

"He'll think I'm hiding something."

"No, he'll just think you don't want to bore him with your stories."

"Or that it's some dumb excuse, that I made up the whole hospital thing..."

"Sent!"

"What?"

"The text."

"No!"

"You told me to."

"Did he answer?"

"Let him read it first, woman! . . . Geez, he doesn't waste any time: 'Tonight?' "

"Tonight what?"

"Guess."

"Show me that!"

In the message bubble that appeared, superimposed on my favourite photograph (the laughing faces of my three adorable children) and just beside the word *now*, I could read "Tonight?" complete with question mark. I scrolled up to see what Claudine had written: "I'm totally fine, don't worry, it was a girlfriend of mine. I'm really looking forward to that drink xx."

"You put kisses!"

"Only two small ones."

"Now what do I look like?"

"Like a girl who's excited to see him."

"No, I look like I'm desperate."

"You are."

"ABSOLUTELY NOT! I AM NOT DESPERATE!"

"What's the most exciting thing that's happened to you in the past six months?"

"Tons of things . . ."

"The Dyson vacuum you paid for with Air Miles?"

"Wait a minute, you're talking to me about an exciting life? *You?*"

"Yes, me. Because if there was the slightest chance something like this could happen to me, I'd jump on it with both feet. I'd run after him as fast as my legs could carry me. I'm just trying to help you out."

"But I don't need help!"

"You definitely do. You were both naked in your living room yesterday and nothing happened!"

"He fell asleep!"

"But then he woke up."

"By then it was too late, I had to go!"

"You kiss, you slip in some tongue, it takes ten seconds."

"IT'S NOT THAT SIMPLE!"

"YES IT IS! YOU TILT YOUR HEAD AND STICK OUT YOUR TONGUE! THAT'S IT, THAT'S ALL!"

"IT'S NOT MY FAULT ADÈLE WALKED IN ON US!"

"What do you mean, Adèle?"

It had been weighing on me, and I should have been more careful. But it was too late to take back my words, and I was too stunned to invent a story and cover for Adèle.

"Your mother didn't want to go to her appointment, so Adèle came up to get me."

"Nobody told me that."

"Adèle won't toot her own horn, and Rosanne didn't really understand what was going on."

"She mentioned some nurse who was 'built like an ox.'"

"Paratransit doesn't come with nurses..."

Claudine pinched the ridge between her eyes and bowed her head. "Guy..."

"It's not a big deal."

"You shouldn't have answered the door."

"I didn't need to."

She pinched harder. "The little shit!"

"Don't worry, I got my revenge."

"I'm not getting involved, it's better that way. I'm too full of violence these days."

I told Guy that my flock had just arrived and that I'd talk to him later — no mention of when, exactly. It was something a (much-loved) grandmother might say. My family had been the best part of my story, and I wasn't about to renounce it now. He responded with a thumbs-up, just as I'd feared, which I interpreted as his way of sweeping our date into a month of Sundays, where it would hibernate for now, along with my aim to get in shape and my new erotic identity. The fact that we'd earned twenty bucks together and spent a few moments in the same room wearing only towels didn't change much: we were barely at the cheek-kissing stage in our relationship.

. . .

Alexandre and Justin arrived right on time, carrying a planter of burgundy chrysanthemums for the gnome garden, a bouquet of daisies for Claudine (the evening's official last-minute hostess), and a pair of good bottles that would elevate the stew by obscuring its weaknesses and enhancing the taste of already out-of-season carrots. They were dressed, as always, in pretty, colourful shirts that exerted a force like that of pregnant women's bellies, inviting hands to touch them brazenly without apology, attracted by the quality of the fabric, the shimmer of the threads, and the vibrant unfamiliarity of the colours. Alexandre came within three inches of my face: "I like your makeup, Mom." He was so sweet, I wanted to cry.

Much to everyone's surprise, Antoine and Malika arrived in the next minute, freshly dressed and carefully groomed. I should have suspected something—reality never alters without reason—but I chalked their punctuality up to my recent existential crisis, which, if only momentarily, may well have shaken my son and his partner out of the comfortable sloppiness of their domestic lives. It wouldn't last, of course, but I infused my greeting with such enthusiasm I hoped they would see how deeply I supported their efforts.

Charlotte arrived, followed by her friendly invertebrate, with a bottle of blue wine (!?!) and some good news. She had been to visit Simon, our diminutive garden gnome–loving neighbour, and had convinced his family to take one of the cats they'd brought to the shelter. The family's own cat, Potato-B, was going downhill, its eyes forever covered in a filmy veil and its kidneys on the verge of not functioning. Charlotte had explained that they'd be saving the world once again by adopting a "used" cat, and the matter seemed to be settled. They would take whichever of the two was in better shape, and Dominic would drop the pardoned animal off later in the week.

"What about the other one?"

"We can't find anyone who wants it."

"So what are you going to do?"

"Whatever we can, Mom."

Only when Laurie waltzed in (alone, we refrained from pointing out) with a bottle of bubbly did I finally realize what was going on around me — and quite literally "around" me. Drinks in hand, everybody was piled on couches or perched on armrests, forming a circle with me at its centre. Dominic had even settled into a yoga-like pose at my feet. I was like a guru positioned as the sun in a gathering that revolved around me.

"Okay, what's going on?"

They exchanged smiles.

There we were, the choppy waters of the Rubicon swelling before us. I could tell they were ready to defy me and cross it, despite my threats. Children don't listen, everybody knows that. Neither do best friends.

"I said I didn't want a birthday party."

"Good thing, because that's not what we're celebrating."

"Then what are we celebrating?"

"Your unbirthday."

"But it's everybody's unbirthday."

"Mostly yours, since your birthday is coming up."

"No, it's the opposite."

"The rules have changed, Mom."

Years ago, after my children read *Alice in Wonderland* and discovered that the Mad Hatter and the March Hare celebrated unbirthdays, it had unleashed countless excuses to eat McCain cakes in the middle of the week. Life's greatest tragedies—disastrous oral presentations, sprained ankles, best friends moving away—had on many occasions been assuaged with mouthfuls of unbirthday cake. So had a number of funerals. I could hardly blame the kids for playing the same card now, although I had to admit I'd walked into this one like a sucker. They were simply transferring their knowledge, reducing the drama of my fiftieth birthday to that of a failed exam.

"I'd like to make an untoast to the youngest mom out there..."

"...to my BFF, my sister from another mister..."

"...to the coolest of mother-in-laws..."

Laurie winked at me, and Rosanne smiled as she sipped her rosé, her compression-booted foot resting on a big pouf.

"Long live the unbirthday girl!"

They had found the formula most likely to please me, while simultaneously disregarding my wishes not to mark the past half-century. An autumn stew surrounded by my nearest and dearest was, by far, the most brilliant of ideas. My voice cracked with emotion as I stammered my thanks.

I was given some bubbly and ordered not to get up for the rest of the night, except to use the bathroom, or to dance if I needed to stretch my legs. They offered me mini hors d'oeuvres from the caterer down the road—a relief, since I couldn't have borne the thought of them spending the day slaving over the oven—served on cute little napkins, just the way I liked them. They refilled my glass, moved cushions around to ensure that I was comfortable, listened to me attentively, and looked over at me with heads tilted slightly, eyes full of affection. Not surprisingly, the best pieces of salt pork found their way into my bowl without a fight, miracle of miracles. I wasn't even allowed to grind my pepper myself. A birthday—or unbirthday—meal differs from ordinary dinners in that everyone is required to leave their thousand daily struggles at the door and play, with all sincerity, the cheerful and big-hearted guest. That's where the real magic lies, far from any fleeting happiness a store-bought cake can offer. And it was the reason why Adèle, who walked in halfway through dinner brandishing her backpack and fuming "What asshole did this?!" was brought down a peg or two by the room's peaceful energy. She understood immediately from the wink I threw her that the "fucking freak!" comments the patch had elicited were my doing. All's fair in love and war.

My children had the grace to skip the photo montage, sparing me from having to pretend that I didn't remember Jacques behind the camera or see him in the shadows of the doctored snapshots. And really, what could they have done with the handful of blurry pictures I'd kept from my youth? The photographs would only have underscored the gaping sinkhole Jacques left behind him when he scampered out of our story and into someone else's, their own photos curling less around the edges. Despite my superhuman efforts to cling to the beauty of the years that preceded the hole, at times I still tripped over its puckered rim and tumbled in, my hands failing to find any purchase to break my fall. During the anguished nights when I relived what it would take years to digest, the spectre of the envelope sealed in the wall of my old house chased me with its murderous secrets.

While I was busy not being allowed to do the dishes,

I checked my messages and almost dropped the phone: Jacques had texted three times.

First at 6:11 p.m.

Thanks for coming yesterday,
it was so wonderful
to see you. xx

Then at 6:23 p.m.

Surgery confirmed
for Monday morning.

And finally at 6:46 p.m.

I'm just an old fool.

For a moment, I held the phone at arm's length to distance myself from the tumult of the words. The gesture wasn't lost on Claudine, who came trotting over while magically avoiding spilling the wine from her too-full glass.

"Who was that?"

"Nobody."

"Lemme see."

"No."

"Guy?"

"No."

"Then who?"

"..."

"Okay, the old bastard."

She forced her smile wider, at the risk of carving new wrinkles into the still-virginal patches of skin. The venomous words shot out of her mouth.

"I hope you'll tell him to fuck off."

"Something like that, I promise."

I went to the bathroom so I could answer all three of his texts at once: "Pleasure. Shit. I agree." No kisses, no nothing. Antiseptic answers for a clean cut.

Claudine was waiting for me when I came out.

"You know Jacques has just entered the disillusionment phase."

"So it seems."

"And that comes with guilt, remorse, and a whole lotta bullshit that'll make him question whether he did the right thing. But it's all nonsense."

"Uh-huh."

"It's just a little spasm, like in the movies when people sit bolt upright in bed before they die."

"I know."

"He and Bimbo are in a slump. He's having a bad trip, he's putting himself on trial so that he can really wallow in the pain. But he'll get over it."

"I know."

"He'll grind your heart into a pulpy mess if you let him get too close."

Claudine knew what she was talking about: Philippe had made his own glorious return before throwing her out again like a pair of old panties the moment she let her guard down. The only reason the second wave of suffering hadn't been as devastating as the first was that there'd been less to destroy.

"Come on!"

She handed me a new glass of bubbly.

"It's time for dessert!"

The Paris-Brest was enormous—monstrous, even. The crown floated over spirals of praline cream that had been piped into columns. A Greek temple of puff pastry, and I'd been charged with the sacrilege of cutting it into pieces. The crust crunched under the sharpened blade. Pure torture. The rest was spooned onto a plastic plate—all for me. I had let the diet slide for half a century; it could wait a bit longer.

"Okay, Mom, come into the living room."

"Why?"

"You'll see."

"I said no roast!"

"We know, that's not what this is. Come, sit."

They hadn't even begun to recite their lines— Charlotte was holding index cards, Alex a Clairefontaine notebook with satiny pages, and Antoine a crumpled sheet of paper—and already I was in tears at the sight of them all together, shoulder to shoulder, magnificent, thriving, so full of life. Jacques had been right. I raised a finger and Claudine refilled my glass: I could pretend to choke on the drink if I fell to pieces too soon.

"We won't talk about your little quirks, or all the times people thought you were crazy. We'd never be able to get through everything..."

There it was, things were heating up.

"Since it's your unbirthday, we've decided to give you an *unroast*..."

"Uncooked."

"Bloody, even."

"...to remind you—not of the things you've done in your life, but rather..."

Then all three, in unison.

"...of the things you haven't!"

"It's called *Fifty Things Mom Didn't Do*."

"We just picked a random number. A nice, round number. It has nothing to do with your unbirthday..."

"No juicy scenes, no murders, no sex. Sorry, Claudine."

We weren't even past the title, and already they were having a blast. How naïve I'd been to think I'd get out of it. Vengeance was being arranged on a silver platter for Adèle to serve, which I understood by the smug wink she threw back at me. I took a deep breath.

"Mom..."

"Dear Mom..."

"Mommy dearest..."

"You never graduated from college—"

Things were off to an auspicious start. To avoid panicking, I tried to remind myself that my children had a good sense of humour. And that I was self-deprecating.

"—but that didn't stop you from getting a good job and being a role model of organization and hard work..."

"...a slight control freak, like all moms..."

Rosanne asked Adèle what that meant.

"Think Captain Von Trapp," she replied.

Rosanne smiled, satisfied.

"You didn't ever really learn to speak English..."

"...which doesn't stop you from muddling through, using gibberish when necessary. And you know we can translate, so..."

"You never seemed frustrated, even when I wet the bed..."

"...or when I dropped my cereal on the stairs and the milk spilled everywhere..."

"...or when I lost my lunch box three days in a row the September I started grade 1..."

"...or when I puked on the couch after I got buzzed on peach schnapps..."

"...or when I got tired of my bangs and cut them off at the roots..."

"...or when I melted my new tennis shoes by leaving them on the entryway heater I'd turned way up so they would dry faster..."

As they recited their long list of anecdotes, mocking each other — and, though they were treading carefully, me along the way, just as any good roast would — the mosaic of our lives together gradually took shape, coloured by small woes that were no doubt devastating at the time, but seemed funny today. Via their tender words I once again became the mother I had been, in turns exhausted, patient, exasperated, worried, amazed. The accordion-like effect of the emotions bubbling up in me almost took my breath away, just like it does every time I'm overwhelmed with love for them. The exhilaration makes me feel so alive.

"Even though you know you never have had, and never will have, any sense of rhythm..."

"...it never stopped you from dancing."

"You didn't redo the ponytail Dad threw together on the day of my grade 3 pictures..."

"...and you didn't say anything when Grandma saw the picture and criticized you for not doing a better job with your daughter's hair."

Charlotte knew how to imitate her grandmother's

haughty air and scandalized tone, her flapping wrist keeping time with her exasperation.

"Even though you *really* didn't want to, you never made a fuss about getting married..."

"...or getting unmarried."

"You never collapsed in the face of great pain, whether it was death or divorce..."

"...you barely even wobbled..."

"...and only ever in a fitting room..."

Charlotte winked at me. I took a sip, and Claudine followed. My phone vibrated, but I didn't look down.

"You never once disowned us. Even when we deserved it."

"You never ran the other way when your children turned out to be clumsy..."

"...awkward..."

"...messy..."

"...whiny..."

"...lazy..."

"...gay..."

Everybody laughed.

"Mommy dearest, you never once put yourself first."

"You didn't go to Italy with Aunt Francine, your one big dream..."

"My fault: scarlet fever."

"You didn't sign up for Zumba..."

"Our fault: hockey..."

"...and the homework I wouldn't have done had you not sat down with me every night and pushed me to do it correctly."

"We never heard you say a bad word about anyone..."

"...not even Grandma, and that says it all..."

"You never blamed your misfortunes on anyone else..."

"...or on the government."

"You never let us hate each other..."

A flurry of elbowing.

"...or go to bed angry."

"You never let us believe life was easy."

"Thanks for the reality check, Mom."

"You never let us loaf around in front of the TV when there were chores to do."

"And you never forced us to eat tripe or blood sausage..."

"...or Brussels sprouts. Thanks, Mom."

"You never *actually* embarrassed us."

"Uhh..."

"We were just pretending, Mom."

Claudine looked over at her daughters. Adèle paid her no attention and Laurie smiled.

"You never had to stand up for us..."

"...you taught us to stand up for ourselves."

"You never allowed us to ignore the many who were less fortunate than we were..."

"...or to believe we were better than Tom, Dick, or Harry..."

"...or to take our material comforts for granted."

"You never let our fears define us."

"You never took your anger out on other people..."

"...water pitchers and lukewarm coffee don't count..."

"...neither do sideboards, speaker systems, or living room trinkets."

Or car tires, luckily.

"You never criticized us for what we weren't."

"*Almost* never."

A wink from Antoine. I took another generous sip to cover up a sob.

"You never let us doubt ourselves."

"You didn't let anyone else dictate what we were worth..."

"...or who we were."

"Dear Mom."

"Mommy dearest."

"You are *our* mom..."

"...a fabulous mom..."

"...and you will never age in our eyes."

"Behind each of the things you didn't do are a thousand kindnesses, a thousand acts of generosity, a thousand sacrifices you made so we could become who we were, who we are, and who we will be..."

"...stable children..."

"...capable teenagers..."

"...happy adults..."

"...good citizens..."

"That was Alex's idea."

"...who know how to love..."

"...and be loved..."

By the time the unhomage ended and everyone started clapping, I was crying like a baby. I kept all my *oh stop!*s, *don't be silly!*s, *you shouldn't have*s, and *this is all too much!*es to myself. True, I wasn't able to get the words out, but they'd also have cast me irremediably as a rambling old fool—which, judging by the flood of compliments I'd just been showered with, I had so far managed to avoid. Dominic, with his usual sophistication, stuck his fingers down his throat and drowned out our hugging and kissing with a shrill whistle more suited to the hockey arena.

"Time for presents!"

"Oh my, not a present, too! I said no gifts, I don't need anything..."

"Well, that's good, since it's not for you. Sit down."

Claudine refilled my glass as they brought out a massive brown cardboard box that looked like it weighed a ton. On it, the kids had drawn small flowers and animals in magic marker with childlike simplicity. I was unable to identify any of the creatures except for the rabbit, whose oversized ears left little room for ambiguity. And there was no way of guessing what was *inside* the box—no telltale shape, texture, or smell. The animals suggested it had something to do with kids, but...

"I'm going to be a grandmother?"

"Huh? No! Of course not, we wouldn't do that to you before your fiftieth..."

"My God, you scared me!"

A completely tactless comment, since I knew Justin and Alexandre were thinking about adopting.

"Open it."

"Would you please tell me...?"

"Come *on!*"

From underneath the crumpled newspaper I pulled out a board game, various children's books, a Battleship set, a bag of dice, a pack of Mille Bornes (!), a bunch of Legos, a few Playmobil sets stuffed into Ziploc bags, playing cards, several other games, and more.

"We thought it could be for the kids at your school. Since you like gifting so much."

"We bought some of it new, the rest came from friends."

"The UNO's mine—it's even better than a new pack because the cards are worn in."

"We did remove the wineglasses from the Playmobil wedding set. We didn't think they were very...well, maternal."

"We let the knights keep their swords, because we don't know what the rule on blades is..."

"...but not the rifles. Now the hunters look more like explorers..."

"...or conservationists studying how multinationals destroy the earth's natural environments through mass deforestation, backed by corrupt governments looking to line their own pockets."

"Want some more bubbly, Char?"

My phone vibrated. Twice. This time, I couldn't resist.

Jacques.

Happy unbirthday! xx
I saw Antoine yesterday,
he told me. It must
be nice to all be together.

I looked up at Claudine, who was smiling widely.

"Guy?"

"Uh-huh."

Her fingers tightened around the device. "I thought so."

"I'm not answering."

"You won't be able to, I'm keeping it. You don't need it."

"I do. I'm waiting for an important text."

"I'll let you know if you get any."

"I don't want you to answer Jacques."

"Promise."

She flashed me her crossed fingers and thick, tipsy-old-woman's tongue.

"You girls aren't fighting, are you?"

"Oh! Alex! Your mom wants to get up and boogie!"

"Yesss! Great idea! Antoine? Find that playlist. We made one just for this!"

Alexandre and Justin had been taking swing lessons for several months. Watching them dance mesmerized me: whenever they moved, it felt like the floor turned to water and flowers were about to start shooting out of their fingertips. The fact that a woman so cruelly devoid of rhythm could have produced a being with such musical ability is proof of how brilliantly natural selection operates. Alexandre's genes had rejected the rhythmically challenged chromosome I'd passed on to him despite myself. There is hope for humanity yet.

They even convinced me to "dance," letting me believe my feet were moving to the beat, that I was following the music, that my body could be commanded, transformed into a yoyo by arms that pushed, caught, and released me. I closed my eyes so that I could feel the movements without seeing them and experience my imaginary flow without the illusion being shattered. I was buoyed by alcohol and the sheer joy of being loved. I felt beautiful and powerful, unattainable. It was a good

thing Claudine had taken my phone away: I was exuber-
ant and capable of doing stupid things. Which is how
too many bad dramedies start.

After everyone left and we'd moved Rosanne to her
bed—she'd fallen asleep on the couch and we'd left her
to it; there's nothing cuter than a grandmother snooz-
ing her way through a party—I went out back with
Claudine to watch her smoke. The cigarettes were on
the secret shelf above the microwave, waiting patiently
in their pack to brighten her nights of excess. Although
I felt nauseous whenever I tried to smoke, I did like
the smell, something of a guilty pleasure these days.
Cigarettes reminded me of my mother, and of the hazy
comfort of our little kitchen on $14^e$ Rue—the Formica
table, the double-butter mashed potatoes, the nights
we spent watching TV and laughing at the bad acting
in our favourite soaps. Whenever I happen to fall in
step behind a smoker, I make sure to walk directly in
their wake, granting me a trip back in time that costs
nothing beyond a few minutes tipped into life's big pot
of small regrets.

"Adèle's staring at us. She's giving us the evil eye . . .
Shit! She's coming over."

The balcony door slid open with a *whoosh* and sucked
it all in.

"ARE YOU KIDDING ME? YOU'RE SMOKING A
CIGARETTE?!"

"Well, I'm not eating it."

"What about cancer?"

"I smoke once in a blue moon, it doesn't count."

"You could still get cancer."

"Then I'll get cancer."

"Who do you think's gonna take care of you? Who's gonna pay for your chemo, your wigs, your hospital bills?"

"The same people who'll have to pay for your brain cancer."

"Oh please!"

"It was in the paper. More than four hours a day spent messing around on Instagram, Tik Tok, and the rest of those crappy apps will turn your brain into pile of white mush."

"And you think you're funny..."

*Shhhhhhlack!* The whole balcony shook from the force of it. The building was still vibrating when the door opened again.

"AND YOU'RE NOT NINE METRES FROM THE DOOR!"

Re-*shhhhhhlack!*

"I know what you're going to say. That I shouldn't let her talk to me like that, and *blah blah blah...*"

"I didn't say anything."

"That child drains me."

"She doesn't want you to get cancer. She loves you.

Plus, she's old enough to ask to live with her dad full-time, and she hasn't."

"Speak of the devil . . . Philippe has a new girlfriend."

"Seriously? Not another student, I hope?"

"Her name's Carole."

"Oh! Then she's got to be at least fifty . . ."

"I think that outside of a university setting, where he's in danger of getting into some serious trouble, he's limited to women more his age."

"Poor Phil, what a fall from grace . . . Okay, give me back my phone."

"Jacques texted *again* around eleven to say he hoped you had a good night. I'm not sure what he was expecting, that shit-for-brains asshole . . . I deleted the conversation. And I erased him from your contacts. I was this close to sending a big all-caps FUCK YOU."

"Why not take him out, while you're at it?"

"It crossed my mind, but I don't have the money."

"I think he was just trying to be nice."

"*Nooo way!* Your ass-chasing ex-husband is *not* just trying to be nice. I talked to Char earlier."

"Char?"

"He and Bimbo are on a break."

"Yeah, that was my impression."

"And sweetie pie isn't just off on some beach catching rays. They're having time apart to 'think about things.' And you know how these things end as well as I do."

The thought of Jacques annihilating our marriage —
and my life — for some whirlwind romance that didn't
even last two years made me dizzy. The innumerable
wounds of the separation and subsequent reconstruc-
tion had ground my family to bits. And all for what?
For a B-movie romance that was cliché, trite, overused:
a handsome older man, an assistant spooked by her
biological clock, a boring and oblivious wife, a well-
timed conference, a divorce, a baby, a flagging passion... another big flop. An epic love story swept away
by what was quickly boiling down to a stale affair, a
bottle of champagne popped too soon.

The Shitmans were keeping vigil in the sanctuary of
their garage, the warm breath of a friendly space heater
far more efficient than any donkey or ox. From where I
was sitting, their lives seemed so simple: wake up, drink
coffee, try to fix a car, drink beer, hang out. I waved,
hoping they wouldn't pick up on my envy.

"Don't do that, they'll come over."

"No they won't, they never leave the Batcave."

"Then they'll ask us to come over."

"I'm heading up."

"Hang on, let me give you some croissants."

"Why?"

"I went to Costco this morning. I bought too many."

"Don't bother, I have everything I need. Bread,
cereal..."

"Milk?"

"Uh...yeah. I have milk."

"Don't move, I'll be right back."

Claudine tossed her cigarette over the railing and dashed into the house. The glowing tip floated on the breeze before settling in one of the heaps of dead leaves strewn about the parking spot. I thought of the celebrity homes engulfed by the flames of California wildfires and of all the grapes whose divine nectar would never comfort broken hearts or soothe weary souls. Claudine reappeared two minutes later, shopping bags in her arms.

"I gave you a box of juice."

"I don't drink juice."

"They come in packs of three, which is too much for me, and this way you'll have some if the kids drop by. And I gave you a carton of raspberries—they come in crates of six, and we won't get through them all before they go bad. And half a Brie de Portneuf, their cheese rounds are as big as Frisbees—oh, and a tub of cretons."

"Cretons?"

"They come in packs of two."

"I don't eat cretons, they remind me too much of dog food."

"Then close your eyes, they're good on Melba toast. I gave you some of those, too."

"Why do you shop at Costco if everything is too big?"

"It's cheaper."

"Not if you give me half of what you buy."

"I mostly go for the toilet paper. I gave you some of that, too."

"Come over for breakfast, at least?"

"Nah, I only gave you four croissants. They wouldn't go far with all of us."

"What's in the big bag?"

"A box of paper towels for school. If I hear one more story involving that awful brown paper…"

"That's so sweet of you!"

"Go on, go to bed. It's freezing out here."

"Have breakfast with me tomorrow."

"Nah, I plan on staying in bed until noon."

"Good idea."

I threw my arms around her and squeezed hard.

"What a perfect night. Thank you so much."

"You're welcome so much. Your kids are…*pfff*… incredible."

"There've been moments I wanted to slit their throats."

"I know."

I walked up the stairs slowly, so I had time to clear my head. The wind on the second-floor balcony was more biting, crueller. I pictured myself standing on the deck of a ship, trapped in a sea of ice. I let the cold cut through my clothes, skin, and bones and snake up my spine, relishing the thought of a hot shower ahead. I was luckier than any frostbitten sailor could ever hope to be.

I reread my text history, checked the news, and sent a message to Charlotte.

I'll take the other
sick cat, it will
be good for Steve.
If it isn't too late.
Two cats in bad shape
might understand each other.

# 12

## In which I lie a little
## and discover a new erotic identity

It wasn't even 7 a.m., and I was sitting in the coffee shop down the street staring at my latte, its milk foam sculpted into a type of heart-shaped fern by a barista brimming with the pep of a camp counsellor. My new schedule had imprinted itself into every cell of my body and I couldn't sleep in any longer, not even on weekends.

I looked up from the paper I'd been reading—the headline claimed that a large number of nursing home residents wind up choking on grilled cheese (!?!)—and let my eyes wander to the bay window and anything that moved beyond it. I made a quick assessment: dog owners are early risers. Suddenly, holding the leash of a magnificent red golden retriever, appeared...

Miss Sophie. Wearing sweats, hair uncombed, looking impossibly pretty for someone who didn't give a damn. If I'd kept my nose buried in the paper like the only other two people in the café, she could have come in behind me, ordered coffee, and left unnoticed. But there I was, all smiles, my eyes riveted to the elegant curves outlined by her fleece. She tied her dog to the bike rack, pointed to the counter—*Hang on a sec while I order*—then came over. I opted for the traditional question, given the circumstances.

"Hey! So, do you live around here?"

"Uh...not really, no."

"Oh?"

"You?"

"Yes, I'm two streets over. I own a duplex with a friend. I live up top..."

She gritted her teeth and glanced around, as if someone were spying on her.

"Your dog is beautiful!"

"He isn't mine."

"Oh. Do you have time to sit down?"

Naturally, the conversation turned to school, kids, Célyane's fabricated stomach aches, Julia's unnamed issue—her parents refused to let her see a specialist and wouldn't accept any sort of intervention—and to Devan, obviously, as she smacked her forehead. She loved her job and wouldn't trade it for anything, she said, despite the meddlesome parents and the increased accountability. While we were chatting, the barista came over and slid two coffees to go in front of Sophie with a "Voilà! Voilà!" I asked no questions (this was one of my talents), but it was fairly clear that the second cup was for the dog's owner, who, unlike her, lived in the neighbourhood.

"Are you married, Diane?"

"Uh...no. Not anymore. I've been divorced for a year and a half."

"Kids?"

"Three. They're adults now."

"How long were you married?"

"Twenty-five years."

"Wow! Twenty-five? How old are you?"

"I was young when we were married."

"Like, twenty?"

The math (20 + 25 + 1.5 = 46.5) added up to a compliment. What a lovely gift for the day after a fiftieth unbirthday. I accepted it without embarrassing myself by tripping over the truth.

"Like that."

"How'd you do it?"

"Do what?"

"Stay with the same man all that time?"

"Hah! Are you married?"

"No, no, definitely not. I..."

She put a hand to her stomach, took a deep breath, and stared into the distance. I imagined the worst: cancer, bruising, stillborn children.

"Things with me are complicated."

"I figured as much, after the whole purse episode..."

"And it's killing me."

"Oh?"

"I can't leave him...but I can't stay, either."

"Leaving is always an option."

"We've been together forever. We have the same friends, the same memories, loving parents, a house, the whole package..."

"People will understand, and you can always sell a house. I know a good real estate agent..."

"We're supposed to be trying for kids."

"Oh."

"But I don't want to. Not with him, not his kids. I'm still taking the pill in secret. Every month he tries to console me for a grief I don't feel. He's so full of hope..."

She choked up, then ran a hand through her hair as if to take back what she'd just said.

"It would destroy him if I left."

"Uh-huh...So who is the other coffee for?"

"My sister. In theory."

"And in practice?"

"For someone with a beautiful dog."

"I see."

"He won't find out, I cover my tracks."

"Don't count on it, everyone has blind spots."

In these moments, age matters. Experience rings true. Her chin recoiled slightly as the blow landed.

"You . . . he . . . ?"

"Yes."

"Okay . . . Do you think I'm an awful person?"

"Not really. I think I can even understand."

"You do?"

"Uh-huh."

I put all the sincerity into it that I could. Some lies are harmless.

"I should go," she said.

"I didn't see you here."

"Thanks."

"You can talk to me whenever you want."

"Thanks, that's sweet of you."

She dashed off, eyes teary, coffees in hand, leash wedged under one arm, her tattered heart a prisoner of its finely boned cage. Sophie's man friend would no doubt be waiting for her, the sheets still damp. I thought about the word *lover* and how it sounded so much gentler than *spouse*, which was both too round and too bouncy, pronounced through a big gulp of air. I had been truthful—I wasn't judging her, though I did envy her. It must be nice to be loved by two men simultaneously.

. . .

When I arrived home, Guy was waiting on the doorstep. I hesitated for a moment before heading toward him, head down.

"Guy?"

"There you are! For a second, I wasn't sure..."

"About?"

"Breakfast."

"Oh?"

"We can do it another time if you'd prefer..."

"No, no, breakfast, of course...I just went for a little walk. Come on in."

My house looked like a pigsty (living alone had made me somewhat careless), and I told myself that the beautiful man standing in front of me smelling of spiced soap deserved better. At least a girl who'd showered.

"Coffee?"

"Are you sure?"

"Of course, come in! Just don't look, I haven't done my housework."

"I won't stay long."

"You can stay as long as you'd like, I...I don't have any plans, I mean..."

Suddenly, all the motions I would ordinarily have managed with my eyes shut were trials: I'd forgotten how to grind coffee and froth milk, I couldn't find the mugs or the sugar. Even walking normally seemed difficult, as if being barefoot — I'd taken off my old slippers — had an effect on gravity. Goes without saying, I stubbed my baby toe on the corner of the island as I tried to skirt it. I let out a torrent of expletives listing an excessive quantity of holy objects, fists pressed tightly into the pit of my stomach to stifle the pain. Guy put a warm hand on my arm, *Come, sit down*, walked over to the freezer, and without a word, opened it and carefully rummaged through until he found my seahorse-shaped ice cube tray. He smiled and freed half a dozen of the little creatures and then wrapped them neatly in the dishtowel lying on the stovetop, tucking them in like an egg roll. He went down on his knees in front of me and slipped his big, beautiful, rough hand under the sole of my foot, lifting it up to wedge my bruised toe between his skin and the makeshift ice pack. Unlike the houses he built, I could feel his fabulous calming force, the tenderness of his movements, the warmth of his body. The beat of my flustered heart pulsed in my foot at the pace of a slow jog. It wasn't the first time he'd knelt before me — come to rescue me — but I was no longer the train wreck he'd once scraped up off the ground. That had been before. Ages ago. Once upon a time. A time in what felt like the very distant past.

Oh, and we ate breakfast.

. . .

"Hey, Claud, gimme a cigarette."

"Why?"

"One guess. To smoke, silly! I'll wait outside. Bring a lighter, too."

In the crook of the alley, a soup of leaves and dirty wrappers swirled around in a soundless typhoon. It looked like the opening credits of a post-apocalyptic movie. The Shitmans were there, as usual, trying to solve the world's problems one beer at a time. They might not build an empire in so doing, but they would have discussed it at length.

Claudine had slipped her coat on over her bathrobe. The crazy-chic look.

"Holy shit, it's cold! Here's your smoke, lady."

"Thanks."

I lit it and drew a deep puff I forced all the way down into my lungs.

"Okay, no. Still gross. Do you want it, or should I throw it out?"

She plucked it from my hands and flicked it down into the pile of leaves—apologies, vineyards—her eyes full of questions for me. I was far too happy to be nauseous.

"Come on, spill."

"Once I realized you'd texted him, I almost came down to throttle you."

"You weren't doing anything, I didn't have a choice. So, is he dirty? I feel like he's that kind of guy..."

"Just enough."

"WHAAAA! YOU HAD SEX!"

The Shitmans raised their heads, I raised my thumb, and the three-headed hydra dove back under the hood of the car. Under the watchful eyes of neighbours like them, we'd be tough to murder.

"Oh my God! With hands like that, it must have been so hot..."

"Enormous hands. The guy's built like an ox."

"Stop! Did you spend all day in bed?"

"No."

"What do you mean? Did you chafe?"

"No."

"Did he?"

"Nooo!"

"It was just a question..."

"We were hungry."

"Ah! That's what the cretons were for!"

"Nailed it."

"Did they put gas back in the tank?"

"Long live cretons!"

I had lived nearly half a century without ever managing to use the verb *exult* in relation to my body. This did not make Guy an exceptional lover, nor did it make Jacques lousy in bed—I hadn't been with enough men to comment on either man's skill, or maybe even on sex generally, and I was aware that circumstances magnified what had just occurred and gave it the semblance of a near-resurrection. I'd spent many good years with Jacques—that I would never deny. Our rocky separation hadn't *entirely* poisoned the memory. But the current state of my head and heart had transformed the hours of physical connection with Guy into something that bordered on ecstasy. Maybe the chemistry between us had converted all the rage I'd once tried to release with a sledgehammer into molecules of euphoria, who knew? And since I knew the bliss would be short-lived, I wasn't about to deny myself the pleasure. I drifted on the current of my fabulous discovery: having sex is like riding a bicycle—you never forget how.

"Did he say stuff?"

"Oh my gosh, you're obsessed! What kind of stuff?"

"Dirty stuff."

"Oh stop! No!"

"What about cute stuff?"

"No, he's not much of a talker. We kissed, we… Normal things."

"NORMAL!"

"Shh!"

"Fine, forget it… Oh, by the way, there's another happy hour this week."

"At Igloo again?"

"Hey, there aren't a ton of choices for old bags like us."

"I shouldn't go, I don't even work there anymore."

"You worked there long enough, you have a lifetime pass."

"J.P.?"

"I'm trying to convince him to come."

"Still married?"

"Yes. And still just as much fun to look at."

She let out a long sigh. I could tell her thoughts had wandered back to my news.

"I felt so small, Claud. I think my whole butt fit into his hands."

"Seriously? He held your butt?"

"With both hands. My little butt. That's my new erotic identity. Me, totally naked."

I didn't tell her about Sophie because Claudine would have hated her. I needed to forgive her a little myself.

Later that night, Charlotte and Dominic came by to drop off my newest resident. I'd almost forgotten. And what with my habit of naming pets after the first words that come to mind, this one was dubbed Baby Bird.

"It looks like someone chewed him up and spit him out. I've never seen a cat so beat up!"

"He spent his life on the streets. Only don't let him out now, he's almost blind."

Baby Bird padded over to the couch, where Cat-in-the-box was dozing, as indifferent to us as he was to the new furball looking for a quiet spot to do his bell lap — he must have already used up all his remaining lives. The next day, once they realized there was enough room and enough food to go around, the two cats fell asleep side by side, scars touching, like two old souls who had finally found each other. Their younger incarnations would have slaughtered each other, but now they were happy to share — even death, which wasn't far off.

Two weeks later, Madeleine was accepted into a seniors' residence for assisted living. Her ninety-three tomatoes and delicate health helped earn her priority on the list. And the idea of eating a hot meal every day had totally won her over, even if it meant having to give up the cats. The fact that the older two had already been adopted led her to believe the others would be fine. I set her up with Stéphane, my savvy real estate agent, who was as soft and comforting as a cashmere shawl. He had orchestrated and single-handedly managed a bidding war between contractors intent on bulldozing the place and throwing up a nice stack of pricey condos. Far too pricey for Madeleine, of course.

# 13

## In which I make
## two important discoveries

The secretary was on the phone struggling with a
difficult parent when I walked in. She put a hand
over the mouthpiece and blew an unruly section of pink
hair from her eyes.

"Have a seat. The principal wants to see you."

"Why?"

"I dunno. Ma'am...yes ma'am...no ma'am...every
class goes outside...no, not when it's pouring, we're not
total idiots...if it's drizzling? Yes, the kids still go out,
it's fall and we can't sit around waiting for a dry day...
listen...no, no exceptions, everybody goes out...it's
even more important when they're little...yes, they
get dirty, that's what a washing machine is for...no,
the principal will say the same thing, but she might

not be as nice . . . Go ahead, call the school board, be my guest . . . call the Ministry while you're at it . . . uh-huh . . . *La Presse*? Sure, open that can of worms . . . My name? Lucie Berthiaume. That's right!"

*Schlack*! She swore under her breath, but kept the edges rounded.

"I mean, seriously! What a piece of work! She wants her kid coming home from school as clean as when he arrived! Does she want him coming home just as dumb, too? I'll give her a clean kid . . . No, but really, get with the program!"

"Did the principal say why she wanted to see me?"

"I had a parent on the line, the hand-soap guy waiting for me to sign off on the delivery, a couple of kids in here, one sick and the other lost — and I mean *really* lost. He was at the wrong *school*, can you believe it?! His mother's boyfriend, for the win . . . The guy leaves him at the entrance like, 'Bye, kiddo, have a good day!' Boyfriend must be new, and the kid didn't see it coming, had no idea this was the wrong school. A kindergartener, only five years old, poor kid, but not real bright. The janitor found him in the hallway after the bell rang, and a good thing, too. I was up to my eyeballs registering a new family with three kids — it's the middle of November! But I know, we don't always choose these things. So nope, the principal didn't say what it was about."

"Okay."

"Have you had your evaluation yet?"

Over time, I'd realized that Lucie was as overwhelming as she was efficient. One quality fed the other. She had no filter; what you saw was what you got.

The yogurt she'd stirred was sitting on the desk, getting warm.

"Yes, I had it last week."

"And?"

"She said she'd clone me if she could."

"Then relax, maybe she just wants to give you a raise."

"Hah!"

Charlotte had been right. Once my feet hit the ground it hadn't taken me long to realize that school went hand in hand with a bunch of very noble words the Machine strove to highlight so it could keep words like *salary* or *paycheque* in the shadows. People are appalled when such words slip from the mouths of elementary school teachers — "She said *what*?!" (the pronoun invariably feminine) — whom we expect to offer themselves up without counting.

The principal gestured at the chair with a complicit half-wink, leading me to believe I might not be in trouble after all.

"Have a seat, Diane."

She plopped down next to me, into the second parent's chair. She looked as if she could have used an expensive kale smoothie with chia seeds and extra protein powder, as well as jumper cables and a week-long vacation to some unexplored exotic island far, far away (somewhere without malaria). Evidently, she was no longer trying to hide the big purple shadows that ballooned beneath her bloodshot eyes.

"Tell me, at dinner do you usually eat your least-favourite thing first?"

"You mean like Brussels sprouts?"

"Uh-huh."

"I used to. But now that I live alone, I only cook things I like to eat."

"If I could only do that with school... Well, now. I've received a complaint."

"A complaint?"

"Against you."

"Against me? From whom?"

"Someone very brave who signed it 'Anonymous.'"

"What are they upset about?"

"It says 'inappropriate conduct in front of students.'"

"Inappropriate? *Me*?"

"For 'getting too close to another employee during school hours.'"

I sucked in all of the air in the room and tightened my fingers around my purse. Ever since our historic breakfast, Guy and I relished running into each other in the hallways "accidentally," touching hands inadvertently, devouring each other with our eyes, mouthing

words of affection to each other from across the yard—
and, on one occasion, even making out hungrily in
what we believed was a hidden corner, like teenagers
starved for contact.

"I imagine you know what I'm talking about?"

"Well, it's just that..."

"Given that it's pretty damn near clear who the complaint is coming from—"

"...but I didn't think..."

"—and this person will jump through hoops to stir
up trouble—it hasn't always been the case, but not
everyone finds ageing easy—I'm ready to shelve it. A
little more discretion and we'll call it a day, okay? The
complaint didn't come from a student or a parent, so it
can stay between us."

"I...Okay, thank you. I guess you're not allowed to
say who..."

"No, but Kathleen is back at it with her damn strap
that's too long."

"Well, that's ridiculous..."

"I'm sending out an internal memo saying we're officially permitting it, along with any other strap the parents deem necessary. We'll announce the good news in
the next *Info Parents* newsletter. We don't have enough
good news, so there's no reason we should keep it to
ourselves. Maybe it'll inspire other parents...there's a
nice broom closet on the second floor I've been meaning

to turn into a bookcase. But the real reason I wanted to see you was to make an offer."

"Oh?"

"I've had two orphaned classrooms running on substitutes since the beginning of the year, I have a sick leave coming up in grade 5—can't say anything more than that—and I've gone through all the names in the candidate pool. We need substitutes like you wouldn't believe. I'm not going to lie; we'd take just about anybody with a degree and a heartbeat."

"Thanks."

"You know what I mean."

"I never finished my degree."

"We can get around that to put you on the substitute list. And you were planning to finish your degree anyway."

"Not really."

"Sure you were . . . I need someone for my grade 1C. I have parents on the verge of a nervous breakdown, and I get it. The kids have gone through four different teachers since the beginning of the year and they're confused. The one who's there now came in here yesterday crying."

"In grade 1?"

"One of the kids called her a dirty old cow."

"Yikes!"

"Exactly."

"They repeat things they hear."

"And that's the worst part, because now I'll have to meet with the parents and come up with an individual education plan, since this is not the first time it's happened. But none of that will matter, because the educational psychologist is booked tighter than Madonna."

"I thought you said you needed a *substitute*..."

"Substitute teaching is like maple taffy, it stretches."

"I can't."

"Just give me a few weeks."

"I won't be able to manage."

"A few days, then. It'll be easier to fill the aide position than to find a sub."

"But I'm not familiar with the materials, with the curriculum..."

"Fabienne will coach you. She's the grade 1B teacher, a real saint. Have you met her?"

"I don't have the patience."

"You've had children, Diane."

"I have, and I'm tired. And I only had three, not twenty-five."

"Twenty."

"Same difference."

"You don't have to wipe and feed the kids. Not much, anyway."

"I'm a little too old to start teaching now."

"Too old? Come on, how old are you?"

I watched as she narrowed her eyes—I was in my mid-fifties, by her calculations. I wanted to tack on a few years so she'd let me off the hook a little easier, but I remembered she had access to my file.

"Late forties."

"Late forties? Diane, that's young!"

"Age is very relative."

"Okay, listen. I just begged the sub to finish the week and asked my mother to light a few candles at church. That should give you some idea of how desperate I am. Please, will you think about it?"

"I couldn't do that to my kindergarteners."

"You're not changing schools."

"But I wouldn't see them anymore!"

"You'd see them less."

"They're so fragile..."

"Miss Sophie is solid, that'll make up for it."

"True. But sometimes life..."

"We can't lose Miss Sophie."

"I know."

"Think of the cash."

"The cash?"

"That was a joke."

Dazed, I walked out of the room. Busying, supervising, and educating twenty fresh little heads all day, every day, seemed, at the moment, an impossible and Herculean task. Even more terrifying was the thought of the forty or so parents (or up to eighty, counting blended families) thirsty for daily briefings and detailed progress reports, and with whom I'd need to negotiate every detail, if I were to believe the complaints I heard Miss Sophie whispering repeatedly under her breath. I had seen for myself that a number of parents, due to some generational shift in the earth that had completely eluded me, seemed to have changed sides (Éléonore's father notwithstanding). Once teachers' natural allies, some parents had become their perfect enemies.

But whatever thoughts I had would have to wait. Sitting in front of Lucie on a little plastic chair, arms crossed over her stomach, Célyane was playing sick. One side of her dress's collar was folded inwards.

"What're you doing here, Célyane?"

"My tummy hurts."

"Again? Show me where."

"Everywhere."

"*Everywhere* everywhere?"

"Yup."

"Like yesterday?"

"It hurts more."

"Okay."

Lucie shrugged. "I tried to call her mother, but she isn't picking up. Poor girl winds up here three times a week complaining of a stomach ache. It's gotta be something chronic."

"Yeah, I think it's pretty common. But luckily it isn't contagious: *n-e-e-d-s a-t-t-e-n-t-i-o-n*."

Célyane wasn't a genius like Devan, and she didn't know how to read yet. In fact, she was one of the few in class who were still unable to write their names — even in wobbly letters. The *y* didn't help things.

"Oh! I see."

"Tell me, Célyane, what was your favourite toy in that big gift box we received?"

"Uh...the Playmobil wedding."

"Oh? And why is that?"

"There's a cake. And tiny plates."

"Can you put the little pieces together to make the big cake?"

"Yesss! And I put the presents on top!"

"Do you like presents?"

"Yesss!"

Her hands had let go of her stomach and were now clasped in prayer.

"What will you ask Santa Claus for this year?"

"A Playmobil wedding."

"But you already have one here!"

"Lucas always takes it. He puts it in his garbage truck."

"What does he put in the garbage truck?"

"Everything!"

"The people, too?"

"Yeah, and the cake..."

She was twisting her fingers, making big circles in the air. Even though most marriages ended in the garbage truck, she didn't need to know that yet. I could preserve her innocence a little longer.

"It'll be your turn next. We'll set up a rotation, and I can come play with you."

"With the Playmobil wedding?"

"Sure, if it doesn't cause any problems, okay?"

"Okaaaay!"

"Want to do tip-tap-toe?"

She jumped up, arms out, elbows bent, one palm up and the other down. Although my brain wasn't what it once was, I'd still managed to learn some hand games with bizarre chants. Gone were the days of Slide and the adventures of Miss Mary Mack. Now the words were disarticulated syllables that bounced off tongues and formed unintelligible mantras, the hand motions accompanying them just as strange.

"Tip-tap-toe, walla walla dum dum, flic-flac-floe, chicka chicka bum bum, pit-pat-poe, basta rasta pump um! Bidi bidi boo, bidi bidi ba... stop!"

I didn't need to let her win; she had my thumb pinned before I could even react. As my joints weakened, so did my reflexes.

"How's your tummy? Does it feel any better?"

"Um..."

"Sure looks like it. Come on, I'll bring you back to class."

"No, we're in the gym."

"Ah, the gym! I see ..."

*Needs attention* or *allergic to gym class* — the jury was still out.

I had agreed to go to dinner with Jacques. Claudine would have killed me if she knew, so I used the happy hour at Igloo ("I'm seeing Guy, I can't go!") to slip out of the house all dressed up without having to field a million questions. He had worn me down with his sweet-talking, charming invitations wrapped in a subtle sense of humour (one had even arrived handwritten on some kind of papyrus), and a doggedness full of half-veiled tenderness. It was disappointing, though not surprising, to see my resistance crumble so easily. I confided in Charlotte, who thought cordiality two years after separating was evidence of wisdom, nothing more. Especially now that ... well, Guy. Choosing your confidant is a way of choosing what you want to hear.

I wish I could say that I'd accepted the invitation to shut him up, to buy peace, to show him I'd moved on, even though I would never entirely forgive him. But it was more complicated than that. I was curious to see exactly where he was in his confusion, how far he would go to get me back—if that was his plan—and, in spite of myself, I wanted him to lay his cards on the table, strip down naked, grovel, and generally suffer a bit. But worst of all, I wasn't entirely confident that I'd be able to resist if he tried to win me back with even the slightest bit of effort. It was a lamentable state of affairs that Claudine was sure to figure out, which meant I needed to lie.

The restaurant Jacques had chosen in the Old Port was very similar to our favourite one back in the day. Blindfolded, I wouldn't have been able to tell the difference—the atmosphere, the music, even the aroma transported me to the cellars of the Saint-Georges. I pulled myself together and smacked the counter with my new leather gloves, as orange as my hair was grey. When the sales assistant had suggested a charcoal coat to help mute the extravagance of the gloves I'd chosen first, I opted for the apple-green one just to annoy her, and now I had to live with my *eccentricity*. Secretly, I had always loved the word, though I could never give in to its whims. But now it was too late.

"So sorry for making you wait, ma'am."

"It's no trouble, sir. I'm here to meet someone."

"Yes, Ms. Delaunais, we were expecting you."

"Oh!"

He smiled shyly and bowed his head. This was classic Jacques: the right contacts, the strategic friendships, the money, the restaurants and private clubs you can just waltz right into. Lots of business was settled over dinner at the company's expense, under the watchful eye of servers whose job was to be discreet.

"I'll take your coat."

"I prefer to keep it, thank you."

"Please, follow me."

You could almost feel warm honey dripping from the chandeliers. A gas fireplace stood majestically in the centre of the room, its four sides made of glass, somehow suspended in the air without feet to anchor it, completely surreal. The air slipped under my skirt, its caress chasing away the cold clinging to the delicate mesh stockings I'd specifically chosen to attract attention. Wine sparkled in glasses, mouths closed elegantly around gigantic scallops pulled from the water hours earlier and forcibly brought to the table through the combined efforts of a boat, a plane, and several refrigerated trucks. For some people, freshness is priceless, planet be damned.

Jacques bent over to pick up something that the waitress had dropped, and she thanked him obsequiously. Her bowed head and curtsy prompted him to make a few witty remarks, unleashing his adorable crow's feet and radiant businessman's smile as he ran a hand through his thick locks. Ever the gentleman, his hand twirled in the air to accompany his words, which seemed to delight the pretty waitress. On the table to his left, the thin black neck of a bottle rested against the side of an ice bucket that had been rigged up via an ingenious system of carved spindles. No doubt the bubbles were very tiny and had a slight mineral taste, the nectar elegant and bold, playful. Jacques was handsome and would be sweet, would smell good, would prove himself sophisticated, witty, intelligent, and entertaining. A gem. Or, depending, a slippery bar of soap. Shortly after we separated, I would have thrown myself at the chair waiting for me in desperation, gulped down his every word mingled with my tears, accepted any and all excuses, expanded on my dreadful boringness, made senseless promises, and welcomed a new ring with sincere, wholly renewed emotion. But over time, the pain of his betrayal had killed me, spreading its insidious poison throughout my body and, one by one, destroying every channel in its wake. My first discovery: I suddenly understood that there was no returning to this man I'd loved too much and who'd sunk the ship. I'd never believe my handsome engineer again, not for all the sincerity in the world. Nor could I trust him, and his wealth only reduced him further in my eyes.

I slid my little butt onto the chair that, in tandem with my pelvis, had been pulled out and pushed in again, the wait staff being so preoccupied with ensuring

I made the least effort possible. When Jacques had announced that he was in love with Someone Else, I'd watched myself plummet through space, stunned that the chair I'd assumed was dedicated to my hindquarters forever had been suddenly pulled out from under me.

"You look magnificent."

The sommelier hastened over to pop the cork and pour the precious beige-yellow champagne, beaming like liquid wheat, into crystal glasses with complicated etchings. I motioned for him to continue pouring, indicating with my nail, painted crimson for the occasion, that I wanted the glass three-quarters full, *a contrario* to everything he'd learned in school. And since the customer is queen, he had no objections to serving so much to the fat boor he must have thought I was. I'd learned some time back not to give a shit about matters of zero importance, and I didn't give even half a shit now.

"Thank you very much."

We clinked glasses and I smiled. I took a sip, made a contented *mmm*, and stood up. One apple-green panel of my crazy-lady coat—that's what we ended up calling it—caught between my legs as I pivoted. I was far too magnificent to stay—my old therapist would have stamped her feet—and didn't look back, not when Jacques called out to me and not when the alarmed server reminded me I wasn't allowed to leave the restaurant with my glass.

"Call the cops, pops!"

I love rhymes.

Out on the wharf, people were frowning or looking at me with envy. Who doesn't like champagne? An older woman, a tourist I assumed had just disembarked from the cruise ship the size of a city docked up ahead, asked me where she could find the wine bar.

"Nowhere, I'm sorry. These are the last *gorgées* of my marriage."

She looked at me silently for a moment—letting the words sink in, I imagine, giving her brain time to digest the word *gorgées*.

"Oh! A complicated story?"

"No, a boring one. Totally cliché."

She placed a wrinkled hand on my arm and closed her eyes.

"Drink up, sweetie. You're young and beautiful. Men are always thirsty."

She went over to a bench where a paunchy man was dozing with his arms crossed, despite the cold, the noise, and the endless foot traffic. She gave the man a firm smack on the shoulder and he didn't even flinch. I figured he was used to it. Suddenly I wanted to write to my children and tell them I'd just had a conversation in English.

I continued to stroll along the wharf until I finished my glass, then threw it as hard as I could into the river.

I expect it was carried by the current as it sank, bumping into seaweed, bits of wood, and trash floating in the water before coming to rest in the muddy depths. Perhaps it would serve as a shelter for some lost, scared little fish.

I texted Claudine.

Still at Igloo?

You coming???

Fabio's here!!

Seriously?

Come on, I'll flag

Hugo down: a Negroni?

No, a gin & tonic,

St. Laurent.

No goddamn

cucumbers, please.

You got it!

The same half-naked nymphet as the last time gave me her spiel on cocktails and cellphones, pointing to the glass canopy full of oldies who'd just come for a drink. Or two. Or three or four. Her frosted cellophane dress was so tight that, much to my amazement, a thin roll of flesh spilled out underneath her arm. Fortunately, this spurred me to kindness.

"I like your dress."

"Thankya."

I made a second important discovery once I laid eyes on J.P., who appeared even more handsome than usual, if that were possible, through the tumbler Claudine was holding out to me. A discovery four gin-and-tonics gently distilled through the course of the evening until it became perfectly clear.

Toward the end of the night, Claudine rolled her glassy eyes and gave me my birthday present.

"I made us reservations at a stinking cute, cozy little cottage with a fireplace and as much wood as you want, cords and cords of it, equipped with all mod cons, comfy couches, stars in the sky, animals in the woods, and if we're really, really, really good, an aurora borealis over our heads. They're rare, but we deserve one. Just you, me, and a whole case of good bottles that end in *ee*: Saint-Bris, Chablis, Pinot Gris . . . yes, I know, the rule of three! . . . it's only a case of six. I'll take care of the food and everything else. All you have to do is hop in the car and choose the music. Right before Christmas, we'll get the hell out of here. Forget about shopping, we'll give everyone money this year. What do you say?"

I really love this girl.

My fiftieth flew by two days later like an eagle in the sky. I didn't feel a thing. Except Guy's warm hands on my skin. On my doorstep that morning, I stumbled across twenty-four white roses from Jacques — courtesy of the office secretary. He might be more determined than I thought. At the end of the day, I took them over to Madeleine's, where I noticed, to my delight, that she'd put on weight.

# 14

## In which everyone clears out

Rosanne had decided to go home. Her ankle was doing better, and she'd have help from neighbours and from her cousin Hortense. Everything would be just fine. Nevertheless, once we packed the car, the goodbye felt funereal. No matter how many times we had looked up the SAQ in her village online and showed her that it had large quantities of rosé in stock, she refused to believe us. We'd loaded her up with three cases.

"Your neighbours could have taken care of the house."

"Nah, houses need full-time love in winter. A cold spell can bust a nail just like that, I'd rather be there to keep things warm. And I can't stay with you forever."

"Well, at least until you're completely healed."

"Healed? You poor child, I'm like an old jalopy ready for the scrap heap."

"Well, then invest in new parts."

"Keep the spares for the kids, my odometer's busted."

When Claudine went back inside to grab a few more bags, Rosanne leaned toward me and whispered, "Nothing scares a man off like a mother-in-law hanging around. She never brings anybody by, I don't like it."

"She's just taking her time."

"Oh please! How long's it been since Philippe?"

"A while, I agree."

"Something doesn't add up, I'm telling you."

Or adds up to too much, given today's impossible standards. At thirty pounds less, Claudine would be a prime cut. Down fifty, a bombshell. The irrational attraction to a sack of bones with sunken eyes had always amazed me, but the love-life expectancy of scrawny women is significantly higher than it is for chubby ones. If *les Filles du roi* had arrived in New France in the twenty-first century, we'd have been left behind on the docks waiting for the next outbreak of scurvy. Claudine is adamant that even a charismatic butterball doesn't stand a chance against an ineffectual beanpole. I want to believe that she's wrong.

Adèle came down for a hug and a few sweet words.

"You little pain in the ass, don't give your mother a hard time!"

"I do nothing and she's all over me!"

"Well, then do something—you gotta move that butt of yours. Come visit me in the middle of nowhere every once in a while."

"And you, no falling down stairs. And no dying!" Adèle shot back.

"Can't make any promises."

Rosanne's voice was on the verge of breaking. She was a wafer of a woman, crispy on the outside and tender on the inside. I hoped for the two of them that the pieces would hold together a little while longer.

Once the Honda was out of sight, I was left alone with Adèle. She opened the conversation by heaving a big sigh.

"Where'd you get that patch, anyway? I've been looking everywhere."

"What for?"

"People at school. It's, like, really in to put cheesy patches everywhere. Mine rocks."

"You're going to laugh. I bought it at the hospital gift shop where they sell flowers and socks and things."

"Can you order online?"

"I doubt it. The shop is run by volunteers your grandmother's age. They do the best they can, but it's all cash and handwritten bills."

"Grannies and technology..."

"Don't call them that, it's not nice."

"It's just another word for grandmother."

"No, *granny* is negative."

"To you."

"To everyone! Open the dictionary!"

"Not to me."

"Jesus, you're exasperating when you want to be."

"Exasperating? *That's* not nice, it has the word *ass* in it."

"Sometimes I really understand your mother."

"Makes sense. You're kind of like my mom, aren't you?"

She cast me a sideways glance, biting her lip and waiting for me to protest. I winked at her and blew her an air kiss. I couldn't help it—I liked Adèle.


At 6:12 a.m. on Monday, the principal called an eighth time. I finally gave in out of pity.

"Good morning, Lady Di!"

The joke had flown around the building before finally coming home to roost. It was my last and only chance to be a princess, so why not?

"I'm sticking with my kindergarteners in the Before and After School program. We'll see if anything changes next year…"

"Sophie won't be in for the next little while."

"Oh no! Shit!"

"Exactly. Shit."

"Was she the one going on leave?"

"Not even close."

"Is she okay?"

"As okay as possible when you need to take some time off."

"It wasn't an accident or anything…physical, was it?"

"I'm not supposed to discuss it with you, but no, her condition seems to be of a different nature."

"Well, thanks."

"But my other problem is that the new grade 1 substitute took off, too."

"Oh my God!"

"Yesterday, I visited the residence where I had to place my mother."

The signs of exhaustion and madness are very similar, incoherence being one.

"I'm sorry."

"The PSW taking care of her was on his eleventh straight day, his fifth sixteen-hour shift in a row, and he'd just been yelled at for not wanting to come in the next day. The poor guy looked like a zombie. He told me he was thinking about quitting…"

"Yikes…"

"And since I haven't had time to shop for groceries— forget about sleep—I stopped at a Burger King on the way home. The place was dead, all the lights were off, and there was a sign on the door: *Closed for the day, understaffed.* Beneath it someone had taped a yellow envelope marked *Resumés."*

"I know, it's awful . . ."

"I feel like I'm in some dystopian movie where everybody's gone to live on another planet except me. Like somehow I missed the shuttle. There are kids and old people everywhere, but nobody to take care of them."

"Them and the people who want fast food."

"The ones who are too busy taking care of the kids and the old people are the ones who want the fast food!"

"True. And what do you want me to do?"

"Say you'll sub for me until Christmas. It's only a few days."

"What will the school board say?"

"The school board posted to Facebook over the weekend looking for teachers and substitutes. They hope it'll attract some of the immigrants from France, but they'd hire aliens if it came to it."

When I told the kids Miss Sophie would be absent for a few days, wiggling the fingers of one hand to limit their imaginations to five, Devan kicked the trash can, Éléonore burst into tears, and Julia dropped her cards. She didn't even attempt to pick them up, she was so overwhelmed.

"But," I said, "I'm still here, I'm not going anywhere. We're staying in our beautiful classroom with our motivation chart, our sticker system, our chore rotation—"

"... six, seven, neight, nine, ten, neleven, twelf, firteen, fourteen, fifteen, sisteen."

Pavel's very first words whistled through the silent classroom as they flew out of his mouth. He had knelt down to pick up the cards, and then sorted and counted them before handing them to Julia, who hastened to verify his work three more times. His voice was scratchy yet silky, with a singsong quality to it. If I hadn't been so afraid of shattering the magic, I would have asked him a thousand questions just to hear him speak again. "Sixteen" would become our talisman, our way of organizing the universe as we waited for the stars to align and Miss Sophie to return.

"Devan, go pick up the trash can, please."

"It wasn't me!"

"And the papers! *All* of them!"

Laurent's mother was crushed when I told her the news later that day. She shut her eyes and dropped her head, as if I'd just announced that her son had died.

"I was supposed to meet with Sophie tomorrow. I imagine this means it's cancelled?"

"I imagine so. If she can't come in to work..."

"Ugh, what horrible timing!"

"Was it about Laurent?"

"Yes, I wanted to talk about his progress. I have some questions, a few concerns."

"Oh? But Laurent's doing really well. He follows directions, he's a quick learner, and he always eats his fruit before his cheese like you asked..."

"We'd requested a derogation for early entry into kindergarten. His birthday is at the beginning of October, and he's so bright, we thought it would be better if he started at four. But our request was denied, "cognitively not ready" was what they told us, and there's no appealing the decision or getting a second evaluation, nothing. It was a 'No,' full stop, even though we were willing to pay whatever it took."

"I see."

"You can understand how we worry. The diagnosis was brutal."

"But he started this year and everything is going well, isn't it?"

"Yes, but we'd like to send him to a special school next year that has a *highly* rated international program. The students are taught in three languages, and we don't want him to miss his chance this time around. We're about to register him for preparatory courses for the entrance exams, and we wanted to know what to prioritize, what needs improving. That's why it's so important I speak to Miss Maheu."

"Maheu?"

"Sophie Maheu."

"Oh! Right."

"It's so infantilizing to call teachers 'Miss' and then their first name, don't you think? I can't believe the schools even allow it."

"Did you have a chance to speak to Sophie at the parent-teacher meetings in November?"

"Yes, but teachers never have much time to talk at those things. We barely had twenty minutes together."

Twenty minutes times twenty kids makes for a long night of talking about short attention spans.

"And if that doesn't work out for Laurent, what is the other option?"

"*Oomph!*"

"He'll do grade 1 here?"

"Well no, that's not really what I'd call an option. There's nothing worse for a child like Laurent than being understimulated. Kindergarten's one thing..."

Some words land as violently as spittle. I gave her an extremely Adèle-ish smile before turning back to my charges. Devan was waiting for me to play a round of Mille Bornes, and it certainly wasn't any of my business if Laurent's mother wanted him to be recruited by NASA before he turned ten. Éléonore's father, who hadn't missed a beat of the conversation, placed a gentle hand on my arm and lowered his eyes before leaving the classroom to vaunt his charms in other pastures. Tarek's mother and Louane's father also came by to offer what appeared to be their condolences, as if I were suffering some of Miss Sophie's unidentified troubles by association. Their concern for her was sincere and went beyond what her absence would mean for the children. I was moved to tears. Perhaps I had made the right choice after all—a series of right choices.

For the last two days, the guys had been packing up the site—dismantling the scaffolding, catwalks, and safety corridors. This had to be the first time in my life I'd seen renovations completed on schedule. Come spring, they'd roll out their gear in and around a different school one town over—like sailors moving from port to port. At a distance, I watched "my" Guy come and go, mighty and magnificent, without really knowing what I wanted from him.

Baby Bird was waiting at the back door when I arrived, a lifeless nuthatch in his paws.

"No, you knucklehead! Claudine bought you a whole case of soft food at Costco... Damn, the poor bird, just as winter's setting in. Come on, get inside."

He wouldn't come in. Proud of having delivered me a nice fresh meal after my long day's work, he watched attentively as I picked the dead bird up using a triple-reinforced plastic bag. How could he possibly hunt, given the state he was in? No idea. Maybe he had landed on a grandfather bird, like him—I had no idea how to distinguish an old bird from a young one. I didn't dare leave his offering outside and risk offending him. Instead, I walked through the apartment and dropped the bag into the garbage bin on the front balcony. By the time I'd returned to the back to see if he was ready to come in, his rump was already on the bottom stair. He took a few slow steps.

"Baby Bird? Where are you going? Come here, kitty! I'm not mad! Come back!"

He turned around at the sound of my voice and— one steamboat, two steamboats, three steamboats— took off without a fuss. He rounded the bend in the alley and disappeared.


"Yes, I'm fine, you? Great. Listen, sweetie, I don't want to bother you, but I have a quick question...Yes, Guy's doing well...so are the kids at school, yes...uh...do cats act like birds? When they die, I mean. Yes, hiding... Oh? But wouldn't he have felt safe in the house? ...Three days. Like Jesus. He's not coming back, I can feel it... Well, he certainly wasn't pretty, the little guy was such a mess, but there was something really sweet about him... Don't tell Madeleine, okay? Now Steve's alone again..."

Baby Bird never did come home. Neither did my children—though, contrary to the cat's, their absence was much preferred. If everything continued to go well, one day it might be my own turn to play the fun grandmother, full of tricks up her sleeve and family recipes. I could count on the school to prepare me.


Pulse, blood pressure, and weight, taken in chaos by the same garden-tattooed nurse. The whole experience smacked of déjà vu, as if I'd never actually left the waiting room. The only notable difference was the slush covering the floor. Winter had snuck up on us, clinging to our boots and creeping through our houses.

"What are you here for today, Mrs. Delaunais?"

"My breasts."

"They hurt?"

"No, they're just old."

She laughed. The lady was funny.

"You're...?"

"Fifty."

"And you've never had a mammogram before?"

"No. The government website suggests women over fifty get one every other year. And I only just turned fifty..."

"Perfect. Is everything else okay?"

"More or less."

"You can go back to the waiting area, we'll call you when it's time."

I had no desire to wait alongside snotty, whiny children, so I turned left and into the hallway outside the exam rooms. I'd avoid the zoo but still be within earshot when they called my name. And the imploring looks on exasperated parents' faces reminded me all too well of how lonely a parent with a sick child can feel, even in a room full of people.

"Hello, ma'am."

The "oh-so-kind" doctor who had seen me the last time was standing in front of me. At first glance, he did seem kind.

"Hello, doctor."

"How are your feet doing?"

"Much better, thanks. This housewife put on socks and got a job. A real one."

He pinched the skin between his eyes and smiled. Not quite an uncomfortable smile, but almost.

"Are you seeing NFD patients today?"

"NFD . . . ?"

"No family doctor."

"No, just my own."

"Phew!"

"Hah!" he said. "You're one tough cookie."

"Likewise."

"Hah!"

He burst out laughing, as if I'd made the joke of the century. The flowered nurse walked past him, frowning and clearly a little skeptical. Once he'd calmed down, he extended a hand.

"Truce?"

"Truce."

"I don't want to be the bearer of bad news, but you're not going to be assigned a family doctor any time soon."

"No?"

"You're far too healthy."

He walked away laughing, a stack of files wedged under one arm. I almost found him handsome. His dated ideas and air of slight self-importance aside, I bet he was an extremely interesting man. An hour and twenty-three minutes later, a younger doctor called me into her office and agreed to put my ageing breasts through the squishing iron.

"I packed some knitting, a few books, and bath salts."

"We're only gone for three days, Claud."

"Yes, but it's good to pretend we'll have time for lots of things. It makes it seem like we're going away for longer. I even pulled out an embroidery hoop from the mothballs. You bet your ass I'm going to relax!"

We followed the curve where Highway 40 ends and headed straight for the St. Lawrence. Even though

I knew Claudine would peel to the left and continue along Route 138, my stomach was in knots. The steering would give out and we'd plunge into the icy river, the doors would be jammed, water would rush in and we'd drown, slowly, one cell at a time, beating our fists helplessly against the windows. But when Route 138 came into view, Claudine slowly rotated her hands, placed on the wheel at ten and two, and as always, we pulled alongside the river instead of driving into it.

"Guy doesn't mind that I kidnapped you?"

"Of course not, he's a big boy."

"Okay. Is it just me, or am I hearing a lack of enthusiasm?"

"Bah! I don't know if that's the right word."

"Are you in love or what?"

"In love? No."

"No? Shit!"

"It doesn't have to be love."

"No, but love is a helluva lotta fun."

"Maybe. But we can't control these things."

"But we can force it."

"Force being in love?"

"Sometimes all it takes is a kick in the pants. When you have a Greek god in your bed..."

"In bed isn't the problem! It's all the rest..."

"What rest?"

"I don't know, I don't know . . . I'm not fully into it."

"I don't understand."

"Me neither."

"That's so sad!"

"No, it's not! I like him, we have fun together . . ."

"You fuck like rabbits."

"Oh please, he falls asleep half the time."

"Seriously?"

"He wakes up at 4 a.m."

"Then what's the problem?"

"I don't know!"

"Had I known, I'd have jumped his bones first."

"I keep trying to figure it out. Maybe I associate him too much with my separation. He watched me destroy my house, my lawn, scraped me off the ground after you fired me—"

"*I* didn't fire you, the company did."

"I can't get those images out of my head, so maybe that's it."

"Want me to tell you what your problem is?"

"Not really."

"You're embarrassed because he works in construction."

"NO! Absolutely not!"

"Oh yes you are!"

"Are you calling me a snob?"

"You spent thirty years in a family of blowhard

aristocrats with more money than God. That stuff doesn't go away."

"But I couldn't care less!"

"You were married to the boss, and now you're going out with the guy who installs the windows. I don't know, but..."

"But nothing! You're *way* off! Jacques was practically handed his shitty little company. Guy works like a dog for every cent he earns, *every cent*. He gets up with the chickens to make sure those blowhards get their little golden nests! He can do anything with his hands— ANYTHING! Jacques can't be bothered to learn which end of a hammer to hold! He'll blow a brain cell figuring out how to fit a goddamn pool onto a private jet, but he wouldn't know the first thing about building an outhouse! Men like Jacques would be eating mud and sleeping in caves if the Guys of the world didn't exist! So no, I'm not the least bit embarrassed!"

"Whoooa! Someone's getting all riled up..."

"If your next sentence contains the word *menopause*, I'll rip your head off."

"I'm done. But I'm glad to hear you defending the poor man."

We were quiet for a few minutes, watching the landscape roll past us as we let the dust settle. It was a scenic drive, and paradise lay ahead of us in a string of snow-capped mountains. Clumps of snow clung to the shore like milk moustaches. The view was so beautiful it hurt.

"I can't be in love with Guy. I like him..."

"Eesh!"

"...I'm happy when I'm with him, I feel pretty, but on the other hand we don't have much to say. And I get the impression...if I really think about it, when I examine it from every angle..."

"You should never think when you're in love."

"I know. That's the thing—I shouldn't, but I can't help wondering!"

"You were saying you get the impression..."

"Well...that I jumped on the first one that came along."

"Oh Lord! Some first ones are worse than others!"

"I know! I'd love to be completely smitten, but I'm not. And that's just the way it is."

"Have you told him?"

"No, I'm just realizing it now as we're talking. And you don't have to be in love to have a lover."

"He's your rebound."

"I guess...Plus, I can't be in love with Guy because I'm kind of in love—no, I'm not really in love, but I'd *like* to be in love like I *could* be in love with him... because even though I'm no spring chicken, and despite everything that's happened, I feel like I could still—I like the sound of that, 'I could still'...and I think, as long as I'm starting over again..."

"Who's the 'him' in your sentence?"

"I said *like* I could be in love, don't freak out."

"I got it, spit it out!"

"J.P."

"J.P.?"

"Uh-huh."

She didn't bat an eye as she slowed the car down to pull into the Ultramar parking lot.

"Don't take it like that! I just mean that I'm not desperate for a man and I'm starting to enjoy being on my own. Of course, if I had the choice, I'd *like* to be in love— really in love. People treat it as some giant scandal when you say you want to find love at fifty. All anyone talks about is finding 'companionship.' *Companionship*? Jesus, does that come with a walker? *Companionship* sounds like 'We take afternoon strolls and go to the theatre together,' as if sex at fifty were dirty. At that rate, might as well hire a lady companion. She could even do the laundry, while we're at it . . ."

I followed Claudine into the junk food temple, where everywhere you looked flashy signs offered USA-sized combos engineered for cardiac arrhythmia and obesity. Case in point: when Claudine went to pay for her "machine brew," the young woman behind the register, whose contours were already taking on a potato-esque quality, offered her a bag of chips or a pack of any flavour Ice Breakers for only $1.79 extra.

"You couldn't pay me to take them off your hands, honey. But that's not your fault. Thanks."

We walked to the end of the parking lot to stretch our legs and look out over the river, which would soon be covered in a sheet of ice. We could see our breath in the frosty air, and the cold stung our lungs as it made its way down. I hunched my shoulders and stuffed my hands in my pockets.

"Just to be clear, I'm not in love with J.P. That's not what I said."

"Fine, fine, but it's no big deal."

"Oh stop! He's married. I'd never do that!"

"What's *that*?"

"Go after him... hit on him... And anyway, it's not like it's up to me."

"Well, you were ready to French kiss him last year."

"I was not! He was an imaginary rebound — a rebound of your invention, need I remind you — to shake the life back into me. I was never going to French kiss him for real!"

"Not even given the opportunity?"

"I doubt it."

"Ah, you doubt it."

"I'm pretty sure. Pretty, pretty sure, actually."

"But..."

"No."

"Okay, it's my turn: I made out with Fabio."

"NO!"

"At Igloo."

"You did? When? Before I showed up?"

"No, toward the end of the night, when I went to the bathroom."

"When I was there?"

"Yes."

"And you didn't tell me?"

"Just look at your reaction. I knew you'd lecture me."

"Shit! He's married!"

"No he isn't, people don't get married anymore."

"But he's taken!"

"Kind of . . ."

"Shit, Claud! What were you thinking?"

I dropped my arms, and my purse went with them; it flew open on impact, and my lipstick bounced out and began to roll across the asphalt.

"It was just a kiss, it doesn't mean anything."

"It means that he's a total jerk!"

"Or that things aren't going well with his girlfriend."

"It doesn't matter! That's none of your business. Get out of there!"

"I needed a little rebound, too! I'm dying of boredom at work, at home, everywhere! I'm dying! I'M DYING!"

Claudine hadn't had a single fling (other than the ones in her head) since Philippe left her to study the practical intelligence of some of his most inspiring female students. I had no trouble believing she was "dying." It felt like a punch to the gut.

"I don't care if he has one girlfriend or twelve, we barely swapped any spit. I didn't eat the guy. And I might never have another chance to make out..."

"Oh stop..."

"I'm getting older and fatter and squishier, I can't see how things will change any time soon."

"Some men look beyond that."

"Yeah, the ones with cataracts parked in nursing homes."

"Come on, now..."

"I've been alone for seven years. *Seven fucking long years.* I'm not counting, but I know anyway. In my head, I'm only forty. And you, you could shave a couple of years off, to let's say forty-eight. Come on, girlie, get in the car before we freeze to death."

I closed my purse and kicked my lipstick so hard it went flying across the asphalt. I do what I can when there's no sledgehammer in sight.

Back on the road, we headed for our cabin somewhere over the rainbow, where we'd have time to sit around the fire and remake the world, squabble and un-squabble. Just then, my phone rang.

"Yikes! It's Jacinthe!"

"Your sister-in-law?"

"*Ex*-sister-in-law."

"Answer it."

"No."

"Put her on speaker, we'll have a laugh."

"All she'll do is piss us off."

"Come on! It'll be funny!"

"Okay, fine...Hello?"

"Hi, Di! It's Jacinthe!"

"Yes, I could tell from the caller ID."

"How are you? It's been a while!"

"I'm fine, you?"

"Super! Are you at home?"

"No, I'm on the way to Charlevoix."

"Then I'll get right to the point: I was wondering if you could watch the kids for me."

"Eeee..."

"When are you back from your trip?"

Claudine looked at me with huge, terrified eyes.

"In a week or two. We'll see how it goes."

"Oh, perfect! So you're around in early January!"

"Uhh...yeah, but I'll be busy..."

"It'll only be for a week."

"A WEEK?"

"I have an incredible opportunity I just can't pass up, you'd do the same if you were me, I swear. Plus, I reallllllly need this. I thought of you when Jacques told me you were working at a school, which means you'll be off in early January because classes will still be out.

You guys get such long breaks, and plus, what are two kids when you're used to thirty or forty? It wouldn't be much of a change from your usual routine, and you're always making food to feed an army as it is…"

And I hung up. And we drove along the river laughing our heads off, as predicted.

"I have some really great news. I wanted to wait until we reached the cabin to tell you, but I can't."

"Whoa! Did they make you CEO?"

"Oh boy, no thank you! Way better than that…"

"Better? My God…"

"Laurie's moving home."

"No! Seriously? She and her boyfriend broke up?"

"YESSS!"

"YAYYY!"

"But we can't get carried away, she won't stay long— at least, I hope not, anyway…"

"No, of course not…"

"Just until she's back on her feet."

We held hands as we drove, as giddy as Thelma and Louise declared innocent. Sometimes, life can be beautiful.

Under a shed somewhere, Madeleine's ancient cat had deposited its withered carcass as it waited patiently, first for death, and then the runoff from spring rains and melting snow that would break down its flesh and carry it to the river, molecule by molecule, right into the stomach of my sleepy little fish in its crystal coupe. Fish eating cats. The world, in all its beauty, turned upside down.

## Acknowledgements

I would like to thank Myriam Caron Belzile and Les Éditions XYZ for having published this novel in the original French, and, at Arachnide and House of Anansi Press, Noah Richler, Bruce Walsh, Maria Golikova, Alysia Shewchuk, Joshua Greenspon, Lucia Kim, and the rest of the team for their hard work and continued loyalty to Diane. Above all, I am tremendously grateful—this, for a second time—to Arielle Aaronson for her *brilliant* and fastidious translation.

MARIE-RENÉE LAVOIE was born in 1974 in Limoilou, near Quebec City. She is the author of four novels, including *Mister Roger and Me*, which won ICI Radio-Canada's "Battle of the Books" — the Quebec equivalent of "Canada Reads" — and the Archambault Prize, and *Autopsy of a Boring Wife*, which was a finalist for the Forest of Reading Evergreen Award, a Hoopla Book Club selection, and a CBC Best Book of the Year. She lives in Limoilou.

ARIELLE AARONSON left her native New Jersey in 2007 to pursue a diploma in Translation Studies at Concordia University in Montreal. She holds an M.A. in Second Language Education from McGill University and has spent the past few years teaching English in the Montreal public school system and creating educational material for second language learners. She previously translated Marie-Renée Lavoie's *Autopsy of a Boring Wife* for Arachnide.